THE OXBOW DEED

CLEMENT HARDIN

SAGEBRUSH
Large Print Westerns

First published in the United States by Ace Books

First Isis Edition
published 2020
by arrangement with
Golden West Literary Agency

A catalogue record for this book is available
from the British Library.

ISBN 978–1–78541–855–6

Published by
Ulverscroft Limited
Anstey, Leicestershire

Set by Words & Graphics Ltd.
Anstey, Leicestershire
Printed and bound in Great Britain by
T. J. International Ltd., Padstow, Cornwall

This book is printed on acid-free paper

CHAPTER
ONE

The ranch foreman had gone out of his way for a look at this meadow where the new hands, Kingman and Chantry, had been put to making fence. He could hear an ax ringing somewhere in a scatter of timber that edged the deep-grassed flats. As he rode nearer he observed the exact spacing of the holes, recognizing in this the signs of a careful workman. Yet he was scowling when he came upon the man at his labor — methodically bending and lifting, ramming the digger home.

That was Kingman, the older of the pair. It was Chantry on the wagon yonder, just now rolling out of the timber with fresh-axed stakes rattling in the box. Standing in the wagonbed to manage his team, he would pause at intervals and throw down a post, then yell the horses on again. When he reached the place where his partner had just finished sinking the final hole, he jumped down to set the pole in place. And then both men turned and waited in silence as Tom Bowers came up and halted.

They were stripped to the waist, and Bowers marked the pallor that hadn't seen a great deal of the sun lately. In this the two were alike, though different enough in most ways — Jess Kingman showing the spare stringiness of his fifty years, the one called Dal Chantry wide-chested and possessed of a young man's bull strength. Looking at Chantry the foreman read truculence in the stubborn stare, in the jut of a jaw no razor could ever keep free of its dark underlying beard. Bowers turned deliberately from that stare to tell the older man, "You boys are doing a good job."

"Thanks," Kingman answered, and waited. His milder, faded blue eyes held none of his partner's hostility. The foreman considered the hang of the sun above the western ridges.

"Might as well be knocking off now."

"Not yet, I guess. We figure there's light enough to get the rest of these posts set. No need making two days' work of it."

"Suit yourself."

The suggestion would have surprised him, coming from the ordinary run of drifters; but these two were not the usual kind, by any manner of means — as Bowers had already discovered. He didn't immediately ride on, nor did he dismount. He shifted position, the saddle creaking under him. He piled both hands on the horn and leaned his weight on them. He had something on his mind that needed saying.

"Let's get one thing straight," he said sternly. "It ain't my aim to ride anybody — but I won't stand for the sort of thing that happened last night." He saw how Chantry's chest lifted, to a sharply drawn breath. "I guess I'm making myself plain enough?"

2

"Plenty!" The young fellow's reply was clipped and angry.

Tom Bowers nodded. "That's good. I'm trying to run a working ranch, and it's no help to have my bunkhouse ripped apart. So, do your brawling somewhere else, and on your own time!"

Chantry squared himself and some hot reply readied itself to pour from him, but his companion spoke faster. "Look here, Bowers! You'd better save some of it for the man Dal had his trouble with. That Pedersen — he's been set on a fight, from the first minute we come here. He wouldn't let it alone until he got one." He added dryly, "I hope he's happy with what he got!"

"He was up and around again this afternoon," Bowers said. "Favoring a rib, and one eye swollen shut. I gave him his time and got rid of him. You run into that kind, once in a while," the foreman conceded. "Troublemaker that figures he's the only tiger on the hill, and every new man is someone he has to keep riding until he can work up a fight.

"No, Chantry, I ain't putting all the blame on you for what happened; you held back pretty good — or maybe it was your friend, here, held you back. But, damn it, once you let go you never quit till you'd half killed him. Matter of plain truth, you're just mean as hell, ain't you?"

The young man's head lowered slightly. There was a flicker of shadow in the hollows of bunched muscle along his jaws. "Anything more?"

"Yeah — there is, as a matter of fact," the other said, on sudden impulse. "There's something about both of

3

you that's had me wondering ever since you came drifting through. You're marked, in a way that's different from any of them others in the bunkhouse. And I don't mean just by being better workers than them, either!"

He saw the pair exchange a swift glance. "What then?" Chantry prodded.

Doggedly, he finished it. "I mean, that it just come home to me. With that pale skin of yours — you two ain't been long out from behind bars!"

Suddenly Tom Bowers was glad for the gun strapped around his waist. Neither of the men who stood before him was armed, but a hammer lay on the seat of the wagon and he saw the plain thought of it in the younger man's quick glance, and in the step he took in that direction, a hand lifting. Bowers actually pulled his own hand back to let it rest on the butt of the holstered gun, and Chantry halted his tentative move.

Jess Kingman spoke then, in a level voice. "Finish it, Bowers. Now you've started . . ."

Tom Bowers straightened in the saddle, pulling at an ear. He would not let himself be abashed by the danger peering wildly out at him from Dal Chantry's stare. "Why, it's just that I'm minded of a story I seen in the paper some weeks back — about a piece of trouble they had in one of the cell blocks over to Deer Lodge. A fire, and a riot. I recollect something about a couple of prisoners saving the warden's neck, at the risk of their own; and I remember readin' afterward that they'd been granted special pardons on account of it. I dunno,

I just got to thinking you might happen to be them same two men."

"And what of it?" Chantry demanded. "Why don't you just tell us we're fired? That's what you're coming to, ain't it?"

"Fired? A pair that works as hard as you do?" Bowers shook his head emphatically. "I'm not *that* crazy — though too curious, maybe, for my own good. Hell, I'm lucky to get you on my payroll, and I know it. Just forget I said anything!"

But when he would have lifted the reins and ridden away, a word from Jess Kingman stopped him. "One minute," the older man said. "This seems as good a time as any to tell you, Bowers. We're gonna be drawing our pay come morning."

"You're quitting?" exclaimed the foreman, the words jarred out of him. "Just because I guessed who you were?"

Kingman shook his gray head. "That has nothing to do with it. It's just that we've been here awhile. We figure it's time for us to take our money and drift."

"You've been here two weeks!" Bowers protested. A sudden thought narrowed the foreman's glance. "You wouldn't be running from somebody?"

"It'd be none of your damned business," Dal Chantry said, cutting in belligerently, "even if it was so!"

"Let it go," his partner said. "No, Bowers, we're not running. Fact is, we're on our way to someplace and we're just anxious to get there. We only stopped off because we needed traveling money. What we got owing us should just about take us the rest of the way."

"I see." Bowers picked up the reins, scowling. "All right. If that's how you want it. Despite what I said about the fighting, I'll be sorry to lose you from the payroll. I mean that!"

Chantry said gruffly, "Okay, mister. We'll take your word. Now let me and Jess here get back to work while we still got some daylight. We don't figure to leave the job for someone else to finish."

The foreman knew when arguing was futile. He nodded. "I'll see there's hot grub waiting in the cook shack." As he turned to ride away, Kingman and Chantry were already tamping the first of the stakes into place.

They worked well together, these two, Chantry shouldering the largest share of the heavy work and easing it off the older man's spare strength. They worked in silence, for they were men who knew each other well enough by now that words weren't needed for communication. Sunset was still vivid in the sky above the ridges when they knocked off, with their job done and the clean line of poles standing ready for the wire.

Dal Chantry gathered tools and tossed them into the wagonbox and climbed to the seat, waiting there while Jess Kingman wearily pulled on shirt and jacket and hauled himself up beside him. The younger man shook the reins and got the horses moving. As the wagon rolled out on the ranch trail, tools clattering in the bed, he shot an anxious look at his companion's silent face.

After a moment he blurted what he had to say. "Hell! Why don't we admit it, Jess? This ain't ever going to work!"

He could feel the probing look of the mild blue eyes. "What ain't?"

"I reckon you know!" He shrugged. "This whole idea of taking me along home with you. I know, we talked about it a lot, but —"

It wasn't easy to say. He hesitated, scowling, and the older man quietly prompted him. "Yes, boy?"

"Well, you must have seen last night what's bound to happen. Let somebody look slanchwise at me and I'll tear into him. There's something in me — I try, but damned if I can hold it back. And all you're hoping is a chance to make up for some of the years you lost in Deer Lodge. I'd be worse than no good for you!"

Jess Kingman said, "Will you trust me to be judge of that? Your trouble is, you've learned never to trust anybody. The world's put a man-sized chip on your shoulder; this may be the way to get rid of it.

"And don't think you won't earn your way! I'm not so young any more. There'll be plenty for a strong back and a good pair of shoulders to carry. I'd kind of like them to be yours — mainly because the two of us have so much in common."

"What, exactly? Fifteen months in the same cell?" Chantry suggested bitterly.

"More than that, boy — more than you know! You might not think it now, but twelve years ago, when they threw me into that place, I was pretty much of a wild man!"

Chantry could only stare at him. "You, Jess?"

"It's a fact. The first day, I slugged a guard — and ended up spending a good part of a year in solitary. I ruined what hope there might have been of having my time cut for good behavior. But I didn't have sense enough to see that — I just figured I was going to die or go out of my mind, if I couldn't get out of there and home to my wife and my kid."

Dal Chantry shook his head, eyeing in wonder the subdued, mild-natured man who sat beside him. "All I can say, they really must have tamed you down!"

"I mostly tamed myself," Kingman told him. "I got to thinking about the man I'd killed, when the sheriff's posse came after me. At least I guess I killed him. I know the judge thought so; it's the reason why he gave me the toughest sentence the law would let him. And I certainly did some wild shooting, that day — nobody was going to take me without a fight!

"Well, anyhow, this was an ordinary sort of fellow, trying to do his duty as he saw it: a man named Bill Spencer, with a wife and family of his own. No call for him to die, just because I happened to be in trouble. When the truth of it came home to me, sitting in that cell, I swore to myself if I ever got out I'd never wear a gun again, or use one. I meant it then; I still do."

The younger man's eyes narrowed. "And what happens when you meet up with that neighbor you told me about — that Luke Blaine? What do you do, shake his hand?"

8

Jess Kingman looked down at the hands in his lap, knotted and hardened by brutal prison toil. The wagon rolled on across bunchgrass flats where dusk already poured out of the timber, while the higher rims still swam with light.

"Maybe you think I haven't asked myself this, ten thousand times!" he said finally. "When somebody's stolen a dozen years from your life, and killed your wife as sure as if with his own hand — how do you forgive him?"

"It's one problem, at least, I *don't* have," the younger man grunted heavily. "I helped stick up that express office, and like a fool let myself get caught — though I ain't saying what might happen if I ever ran across the pair of drifters who talked me into it . . ." He lifted his shoulders. "Well, Jess, you know what you can be getting into, with me along. If you're game for it, *I* am."

"Then there's nothing more to argue about," Kingman said with finality. "We won't bring the subject up again."

So it was, with good horseflesh under them and even a few dollars in their pockets, that these men who bore the mark of prison rode west into country that held cruel memories for Jess Kingman, and an uncertain future for his companion. They kept up a stiff pace. Nearly home, now, Kingman was giving way at last to an impatience he'd somehow learned to discipline. Nights by their trail fires, Dal Chantry would watch him pacing feverishly, and afterward he knew the older man lay awake, long after he himself had given in to the unaccustomed weariness of hours in the saddle.

They weren't even yet in condition, either of them, but freedom was beginning to take the look of prison from their eyes, and some of the smell of it out of their flesh.

Kingman had one of his daughter's letters in his pocket, the last to reach him before they'd left Deer Lodge. Its pages were filled with news of home, and Chantry thought his friend must surely know it now by heart — how the grass had never been richer along the Oxbow meadows, how the house and the other ranch buildings looked with their new paint and the flowers blooming in Millie Kingman's scatter garden, how the Kingman herd was shaping up with a good fall market in view.

"Cross K's not the biggest outfit in Montana," Kingman said on the last night, "but it's about to start growing now. It's one wonderful girl I got there! Think of it — managing a ranch and a crew, all by herself since her mother died! And finding time to write these letters. They're the only thing that's kept me going.

"Do you realize, she was only a child when I saw her last? I might not even know her. But what a surprise I'm bringing her tomorrow! Well take the burden off her shoulders, boy, that she's been carrying all alone for a hell of a lot too long . . ."

Dal Chantry found something vaguely troubling him. Looking at the fire he asked, "You've never seen your family in twelve years? They never once came to visit you in prison?"

Kingman shook his head. "They wanted to, at first, but — well, there was all that time in solitary . . .

Besides, I was too bitter. I didn't want them to see me in prison, but to remember me the way I'd been before. I was always afraid the trip would be too much for Harriet, the state her health was in. And then it was too late — and she was gone . . ."

His voice, there in the shadows beyond the fire, faltered and broke, and Chantry didn't press him further. After all, he couldn't put a name to the odd premonition that bothered him. Perhaps it was merely sour experience, warning him never to expect anything to be as good as it was hoped for.

But he felt a cold breath of doubt that wouldn't be shrugged away.

One more day, threading rough hill-and-timber range that grew increasingly familiar to the exile; then, in still another sunset, they pulled up on the edge of the Oxbow rim and looked down across miles of grass, and the river mirroring the burning sky. "How's it look to you?" Kingman demanded from a depth of feeling. "Was I wrong? Was it worth waiting for?"

For all his skeptical doubts, Dal Chantry was impressed. "It looks fine," he admitted. "Don't think I ever saw better range. And that's the truth."

His companion showed him a face turned almost young again. "I knew! I knew you'd feel it. It's like I said — we're a lot the same, you and me. We've got the same needs and the same hungers. And the old Oxbow can satisfy them all! You've come home, boy. Just the same as I have. Shall we head down?"

Chantry nodded, soberly. They took the reins, and nudged their horses forward.

CHAPTER
TWO

They came without fanfare across the flats that tilted toward the river as fading sunset turned its gold to beaten silver. "I own some of the best range in these parts," Jess Kingman said proudly. "All this along the near stretch of the river, and the hills yonder for summer pasture. Even the winters aren't too bad, protected by these ridges."

Chantry had been eyeing the few head of beef cattle that dotted the rich grass. "I notice," he said slowly, "they mostly seem to be wearing a Broken Arrow brand. Don't see no Cross K's."

Grainy dusk had begun stealing from the timber, but there was light enough to show the other's frown. "Broken Arrow!" he exclaimed. "What's Luke Blaine's stock doing on my grass?" He added, after a moment, "And yonder's a jag of Heart Nines. That one, I don't remember at all. Can't recall Millie saying anything about it in her letters, either. There's something about all this I just don't understand!"

Chantry said nothing.

They rode on, crossing the river at a swift but shallow fording, and so came to Cross K headquarters at the head of a sloping tongue of meadow. As a thin timber screen opened out, bringing the cluster of corrals and buildings into sight, Jess Kingman gave a sudden gasp. They touched up their horses with the spurs, and approached the place in stunned silence.

It had the unmistakable look of desertion: corral bars were broken and tumbled; the front door of the house sagged open on a black interior; the yard stood hip-high in weeds. Kingman said again, in a lost voice, "I don't understand . . ."

They swung down, saddle-stiff, letting their mounts stand with trailing reins as they went across the yard and up the steps. The boards of the porch sagged on rotted stringers; glass from a broken window crunched underfoot. Night was very near, but enough light remained to show the litter and mustiness beyond the open door.

"Stay here," grunted Chantry, and stepped inside.

His boots kicking aside trash, he went quickly through the house, finding a living room and kitchen, and two small bedrooms opening off them. There were a few sticks of furniture, but mostly papers and moldy litter. On a shelf in the kitchen, above the rusted stove, was a kerosene lamp. It was dry, but he found a fuel tin in the pantry and, shaking it, heard a little liquid slosh about inside. Hastily he filled the lamp, dug up a match and got the wick lighted, blew dust from the glass shade. Afterward he carried the lamp back into the living room and set it on a table, next to the smashed window.

On the porch he found Jess Kingman standing just as he'd been left; the older man shook his head, shocked and stunned past believing. "I don't understand!" he repeated over and over, helplessly. "Those letters — every month, without fail. And all the things she told me: the cattle, the new paint, the flowers —" He gestured toward the wreckage of flowerbeds below the porch. They held only ancient weeds.

"Dal!" he cried in sudden anguish. "*Where's my girl?*"

A circuit of the ranch layout disclosed nothing except further signs of decay and long abandonment. The bunkhouse had no door. Rats had taken over the barn and when Dal Chantry struck an upright with a broken wagon wheel spoke he could hear them scurry in a whisking tide. Some mildewed, rotted harness hung from wall pegs, but there was no sign of usable equipment. The corrals were ruins, and had plainly not held stock in years.

Later, the two men sat together on the edge of the crumbling porch, with the lamp in the window behind them, and they tried to figure this. But it was a baffling, blank wall they faced.

Jess Kingman had aged more this half hour than in all his years of prison. Slump-shouldered, shaken, he had taken that last letter from his pocket and was turning it over and over, as though he would force it to answer his anguished questions. Chantry took the envelope from him, studied the postmark. "Mailed here at Oxbow," he said, "five weeks ago. You're certain that's your daughter's writing?"

"She forms her characters just the way her mother used to."

14

"Then I reckon it's obvious. Millie must have had some bad luck, trying to hold on to the place, and couldn't make it. But she kept writing the way she did so you wouldn't have to know and worry. She wanted to spare you."

Jess Kingman shook his graying head. "You must be right, of course. But — My God! Those letters have been so *real*! Why, I could follow them right through the seasons — year after year . . ."

He was interrupted by Dal Chantry's quick exclamation: "Watch it! Someone coming."

Both men were on their feet, quickly fading back into the darkness of the littered porch to wait as a pair of riders drummed toward them from the direction of the river. They slowed, nearing; the rank weeds whispered around their horses' legs. Seeming not to observe the pair waiting in the shadow of the porch, they halted and there was a murmured exchange of talk — a man's voice, and a woman's. It was the latter who lifted a call toward the darkened house: "Is there someone here?"

"Who wants to know?" countered Dal Chantry.

He walked out into the spread of light from the window and after a second's hesitation Kingman joined him. The woman — her voice held the clear timbre of a girl's — said, on a note of doubt, "We saw the light. We wondered what anybody could be doing around this old deserted house."

"They look like a pair of range tramps, Gwen," the man said. He had a clipped, precise way of speaking; an Easterner, perhaps.

The girl's horse had sidled into the glow from the window and Chantry could see her faintly — a slim figure in riding jacket and breeches, and boots with dime-sized spurs. Shoulder-length, honey-colored curls framed an oval face. He caught a gleam of scar tissue on the mount's shoulder and recognized the brand it formed.

"You're from Broken Arrow?" he demanded.

"Yes," she said. "It's my uncle's brand. I'm Gwen Macaulay. Why?"

"I just wondered if you could tell me how long Cross K property has been run-down and empty like this?"

She appeared puzzled. "Why — always, so far as I know. Of course, I've been here on the Oxbow only a little more than a year, myself. I don't know an awful lot about this section of our range . . ."

"*Your* range?" he echoed, sharply.

The Easterner caught him up in an angered voice. "That's what she said. Are you trying to make her out a liar?"

Chantry held back a retort. "I'm just trying to get some information. It's pretty baffling for a man to come back after a dozen years and find his home a wreck, his family gone, and his grass claimed by another brand's cattle!"

"This is you?"

"Not me." Dal indicated the graying man beside him. "Jess Kingman, here, is owner of the Cross K."

"Kingman?" Gwen Macaulay repeated the name, as though perplexed. "I don't think I ever — But, wait! I do seem to remember hearing something about the

16

man who had this old place. I thought he'd died, or gone to —" She faltered.

Jess Kingman nodded. "Gone to prison — you heard right. But I'm back now, and I want to know about my daughter. What's happened to her?"

"I never knew of any daughter! Honestly!" Then Gwen Macaulay was swinging down from saddle, walking toward them into the lamplight. She shaped up as a tall girl — reaching higher than Dal Chantry's shoulder. He couldn't tell the color of her eyes but they were dark, and they looked at a man levelly. Her features seemed regular, well formed. There was an earnest directness about her that he liked.

"I wish I could help," she said. "If what you say is really true. As I told you, I've only lived on the Oxbow a little while — since my parents died . . . What was her name?"

"Millie. She'd be about your age, miss — only, dark." Kingman peered at her anxiously. "You're sure you wouldn't know anybody like that? Anywhere in the Valley?"

She shook her head. "I'm sorry. When did you hear from her?"

"Just a month ago!" The answer came from the depths of despair. "She wrote that she'd had a new coat of white paint put on the house — that there were marigolds in the scatter garden as big as sunflowers. And instead I find — this!"

Gwen Macaulay's companion leaned from the saddle. He wore gold-rimmed spectacles that flashed in the lamplight and a neatly trimmed moustache. He said, "Appears to me, old chap, this girl of yours must have been feeding you a line. Sold all your cattle, maybe, and ran off with some sewing machine drummer . . ."

"Why damn you!" cried Kingman, and took an angry step toward the stranger. His voice was close to a choking sob. And as Dal Chantry stopped him, the Macaulay girl whirled on the other man.

"That isn't fair, Clyde Humbird! You never knew the girl; you have no right to say such things about her!"

"I stand corrected," the Easterner murmured, inclining his well groomed head. To Jess Kingman he said, "I apologize. Naturally."

Chantry, incensed, told him, "It just might be a good idea, mister, if you kept your mouth shut — and your horn out of business that don't concern you."

"Since Clyde Humbird may soon become my uncle's partner in the Broken Arrow," Gwen Macaclay told him, crisply, "all this may be some of his concern. I could ask how about yourself. Just who are you?"

That was a fair question, and there was no use evading it — or lying. "You've probably guessed already," he said. "I'm just another damned jailbird. Jess and I were cellmates that happened to get pardoned at the same time. We came here to take over the Cross K — only, we seem to find somebody else claiming Cross K range."

"Why don't you come to Broken Arrow," the girl suggested, "and talk to my uncle? Surely this can all be straightened out."

Dal Chantry said bleakly, "Don't worry! We'll be looking Luke Blaine up, all right! But our first job is to try and find some clue toward this missing girl."

"I see . . ." It seemed to leave little more to be said, and Gwen Macaulay turned slowly to her waiting horse. She swung lightly astride, and then reined back to look down from the saddle.

"I hope you find her," she said gravely. "I honestly do!"

Jess Kingman nodded, in answer. "Thank you, miss."

After that the pair moved into the darkness; the men stood and listened to the hoofsound swell and fade, running out along the grass flats before they were lost in silence.

They turned back then to the house.

CHAPTER
THREE

"Old building's sound enough," Dal Chantry said. "It's just been criminally neglected. Every tramp that's crossed this range must have made camp in it, and the stock has been wandering in and out for years, But if we pitch in, maybe we can get the filth cleaned out enough tonight to make it livable — one or two of its rooms at least."

The older man shook his graying head, disconsolately. "I want to look for Millie! You don't suppose Luke Blaine could have done something to her?"

"We'll find out. We'll go into town tomorrow and talk to the postmaster. After all, he'll be able to tell us how those letters get posted. So, you see, there's no real mystery. Meanwhile, we got to have the place in some shape when we do find your girl, and bring her home to it."

Kingman nodded. "I suppose you're right."

"Then let's get after some of this litter!" It appeared to Chantry — worried as he was about the older man's stunned reaction to this homecoming — that some sort of activity and constructive work to occupy his hands was the best thing now for Jess Kingman, until his numbed brain could recover from the shock.

For his own part, he discovered that the image of Gwen Macaulay clung persistently in his thoughts, even after those few moments but half-seen in the light through the broken window. Perhaps this was simply the reaction of a man shut away from any sight or sound of a woman for too many months; and yet it seemed to him that there had been something in her voice — in the direct look she had — that struck a special chord in him.

And then he felt the stab of jealousy as he remembered the Easterner, Clyde Humbird, and wondered what the relationship might be between him and the girl. But what business had he — an ex-convict, free only on the clemency of a governor's pardon — thinking about any girl, or setting himself in comparison with such a man as the handsome Easterner? There was a real fury in the way he threw himself into the work of cleaning up.

They started at the back of the house, in the kitchen which after all is the heart and center of any ranch house. Before knocking off they had the trash swept out of it, the walls and floor scrubbed down, a broken leg of the rusty stove propped up and sections of stove pipe reassembled. One of the two bedrooms had also been cleaned out, but the old iron bedstead lacked springs or a mattress, and so once more they slept rolled up in their blankets, on the kitchen floor — tired out by their labor, after the days of riding.

They were up before dawn to throw together a meager breakfast from what remained of their trail supplies. First sunlight was slanting across the meadow as they saddled and rode eastward; morning was still young when they rode into Oxbow town, lying at a point where the county seat road entered this valley through a low pass to the south.

"Hasn't changed, to speak of," Jess Kingman observed, as they looked over the cow country hub — an irregular scatter of streets and buildings, the fringe of frame houses straggling up into pines behind the town. "Not near as much as I'd have expected, in a dozen years. But I suppose a lot of the people will have changed."

"Where's the post office?" Chantry asked.

"It used to be in Matt Starbuck's store." He peered around him, trying to get the pattern of the place set again, his mental map oriented. "That would be just off Main Street, a couple blocks up."

They rode along the crooked thoroughfare, through thin morning traffic. Chantry kept a careful eye on his companion and saw him anxiously scanning the few faces they saw on the sidewalks, the signs that marked the places of business. It would be an odd experience, he supposed, and maybe a heartbreaking one. Jess Kingman would have had his friends, in that time so long past. Some of those friendships might even have survived the test of his conviction and imprisonment on a dual charge of cattle rustling and manslaughter. But time, too, would have had its way, and would have winnowed out some of those old acquaintances.

Too bad, he thought with a wry grimace, that it couldn't have taken Luke Blaine. Kingman had said that his old enemy should be well into his sixties by

22

now and apparently still going strong. Meanness when it became engrained had a way of verging on the immortal. It was too much to expect that the man who had railroaded his neighbor to prison would simply die and leave Jess Kingman in peace.

And then Chantry remembered that if Blaine had been dead, in all likelihood he would never have met Luke Blaine's niece. This made him wonder at himself, again; he asked himself why this girl, who was little more than a dimly outlined figure and a voice heard in the dusk, should still — so many hours afterward — create such a stir of excitement in his nerves.

"Here's the place," Kingman said, and they put their horses to the rack in front of a store building. "Starbuck's General Mercantile," a sign above the jutting porch roof proclaimed; there was a smaller one below this that said, "U.S. Post Office, Oxbow, Montana." Chantry stepped down and tied loosely, and then waited as his friend came out of his saddle more slowly.

Something made him look sharply at Kingman and he saw the expression on the older man's face, and the unsteadiness in his hands as he fumbled at knotting the reins about the pole. He realized that Jess was frightened. He said gruffly, "Give me the letter. I'll ask the questions." His friend surrendered it without question, and followed Chantry up the single broad step and across the echoing planks of the porch.

The store was long and low ceilinged, with shelves lined to the rafters with the amazing conglomeration of goods that made up the stock of a country store. A plain wooden counter ran the length of the room and at one end was the wicket and the letter slots of the post office.

A bell over the door jangled as they let the screen swing to behind them. A woman's hearty voice called from beyond an inner door that led, probably, to a stockroom: "Be with you in a minute, out there." Chantry walked slowly down the room to the wicket, Kingman trailing him.

As they reached it the woman came shouldering past the stockroom door carrying a carton of canned goods, which she deposited on the counter and then moved briskly down the other side of the counter, brushing dust from her hands. She was a capable-looking person, strong and deep-bosomed, with candid brown eyes and hair that was beginning to streak with gray. She shoved back a few strands that had fallen during her labors in the stockroom and said, pleasantly, "Well, young man?"

Chantry placed the envelope on the counter and pushed it toward her, through the wicket opening. He said, without preliminary, "We'd like to know what you can tell us about this."

The woman's stare settled on the envelope, and rested there a long moment. She did not bother to pick the thing up; she seemed to recognize it readily enough. Eyes in a face gone grave lifted sharply to Chantry's, and then past him as she seemed to catch sight of his companion for the first time. The eyes widened. "Jess Kingman!" she gasped.

The latter nodded, soberly. "Hello, Ada."

"But, what in the world — ? How — ?"

"It's legal," he said. "They turned us loose, Ada." And then, as she began to turn red, he added, "This is Dalhart Chantry — a friend of mine."

"Oh!" The brown eyes returned to Chantry, quickly assessing him. "I think I must have heard that name. From Millie."

Chantry nodded shortly. "You probably know exactly why we're here, then. We got in last evening and went out to the ranch, looking for Jess's girl. We couldn't find her. We couldn't find a sign of her."

"Nothing," Kingman put in, his voice bleak. "Just ruin, and empty buildings — and dust. What's it mean? Where's Millie? Ada, you've got to tell me!"

Ada Starbuck looked from one to the other. She moistened her lips with her tongue, and then she nodded and told them quickly, "You step in back. We got a lot to talk about."

Jess Kingman cried, "She — my girl isn't — ?"

"No, no! She's fine. Well, and safe. But —" The woman made a gesture toward a second door beyond the counter. "Just go right through there and into the living room. I'll lock up, so we can talk without no interruptions . . ."

The men exchanged a look, and a nod. Ada Starbuck was already rounding the end of the counter and going over to close the outside door and lock it and pull the shade, to indicate that she was closed to business for the time being. Chantry and Kingman, following her instructions, went through a drop gate in the counter and pushed a curtain aside, and found themselves in the living quarters at the rear of the building.

Here there was the comfortable abandon of a busy woman who had little time to be fussy about furnishings or neatness. A round-topped table with an embroidered runner and a lamp with a decorated shade filled the center of the living room. There were battered but comfortable looking chairs, a sewing machine, a couple of pictures on the walls that Ada Starbuck had cut from magazine covers. Her visitors looked about them, and Kingman had a troubled frown on him as the woman came bustling into the room. He had already suspected the truth, but he asked, "Where's Matt?"

She shook her graying head. "Pneumonia got him, Jess. Eight years ago."

"Eight years!" he echoed. "So long ago as that? It's been a time, hasn't it? I'm sorry, Ada."

She made the gesture of one who had lived with her loss and grown accustomed to it, and had let life grow scar tissue over the wound of old memories. She indicated a couple of shapeless overstuffed chairs that helped fill the cluttered room. "Clear those and sit. Lord knows I'm the world's worst housekeeper — and I wasn't expecting company! Can I put some coffee on for you?"

Chantry shook his head as he lowered himself to a seat and laid his hat on the table. "We'll take a raincheck on the coffee, if it's all right with you, Mrs. Starbuck. Just now we're really only interested in information."

"Of course," she agreed, and took a straight chair facing them across the heavy table. "I can't blame you for that. Millie's all right," she went on, turning to the older man. "She's up at Hermit Flat."

"Hermit Flat?" He shook his head, bewildered. "That's a couple hundred miles. How long has she been there? A long time, I guess — to judge from the mess we found at Cross K!"

"You can figure it for yourself. It was a little over a year after you — left, that Millie's mother was able to hold on to the ranch and somehow keep things going."

Kingman appeared drawn and old. "Only a year!" he echoed.

"She just couldn't manage alone. The market went bad, and she sold off most of the stock and used up what money was left, hiring lawyers — trying to get you an appeal. That failed, and then — well, she had to think of the girl, growing up there on the ranch, amid the talk —"

"Talk?"

Ada Starbuck hesitated and shrugged. She looked definitely uncomfortable under his probing stare. "You know how it is," she said. "A woman, alone with a crew of men, and her husband in prison . . ." She reached a hand and laid it on Kingman's sleeve, as his fist clenched hard and the muscles bunched in his hollow cheeks. "Jess, I hate this like poison — bein' the one to tell you what Harriet went through — but you've got to know."

"It's all right," he managed, after a moment, while Dal Chantry watched him anxiously. Kingman opened his clenched hands, spread them palms down upon the table. He looked at his hands as he went on in a dead and monotonous voice: "You're saying malicious gossip drove her away from the Oxbow. Was that more of Luke Blaine's doings?"

She hesitated just a shade too long. "Who ever does know how such things get started?"

"It was Blaine," he concluded, tightly. Chantry saw the fire that heated up his eyes and made his lips draw out thin, their corners trembling. But then his emotion died a little and Jess Kingman said tiredly, "Sorry, Ada. Tell it your way — I won't push you. Still, it hits a man hard to learn all this, when he'd never dreamed —"

"What could you have done about it if you'd known?" she pointed out. "The way Harriet saw it, you had enough to carry. When she left, she arranged with Matt and me to forward her letters; meanwhile, she wanted to go where she wasn't known, where the talk wouldn't be able to follow her and the little girl. They tried Helena, and Butte, then finally settled in Hermit Flat. It was close as Harriet thought she dared to get, and not run any risk of being found out by Luke Blaine, or the other people she didn't want to see. You understand, she still loved this Oxbow country. In spite of everything."

Dal Chantry asked, "But what was she doing, all during those years?"

"Whatever she could, to take care of the child. At Hermit Flat she worked in the hotel, did some dressmaking. She was always good with a needle."

"She was that," Jess Kingman agreed, out of a depth of troubled emotion.

"She kept a roof over their heads, somehow, and got Millie through school. And always she managed to put aside enough to pay the taxes on Cross K. Millie was sixteen when she died — old enough to carry on the job in her mother's place. Between them, the title's been held clear against the day when you would be home again, Jess, and ready to put the ranch back in operation."

"All those years!" Kingman said numbly. "First Harriet, and then the girl. Keeping up the pretense — never letting me guess, even for a minute, but what everything was going fine with them . . ."

"Strikes me it was pretty damn cruel," Dal Chantry muttered, "to lead him on like that!"

"Cruel?" The woman gave him a reproving look. "It was done for love! As for the wisdom of it, I always had my doubts. I was afraid the blow of learning the truth might fall all the harder, when it did. But it wasn't for me to say.

"Eventually, of course, when time came around he'd have been told the truth. Only, that's not how it worked out! Suddenly the letters from the prison stopped coming. Millie wrote desperately to ask if I had any idea what might have happened."

"I was on my way home," Kingman explained. "I sort of thought word about my pardon would have reached here ahead of me, but if not I meant to surprise her. And instead —" He lifted a hand, rubbed it slowly across his face. Dal Chantry anxiously watched his friend.

"You say she's all right?" Kingman persisted. "You're sure?"

"Millie's doing fine, Jess," the woman assured him. "I've been up to see her any number of times. She teaches school, works in a store during the summer. Lives with a good family . . ."

He dropped his hand on the table, palm downward. "I'm going to Hermit Flat," he said with sudden resolution.

Ada Starbuck looked at a metal alarm clock on a shelf. "There's a stage out this morning. But you'll have to hurry."

"Take it, Jess," Chantry said, as the older man got to his feet. "Find your girl and bring her home."

Still the other hesitated, assailed by sudden doubts. "I dunno. I wonder if I have any right. We've got no money, no hope of stocking the place . . ."

"Take one step at a time," the woman said. "You've got the land — that's the important thing. As for money, your credit's good with me, at least."

Kingman frowned at her. "You have any idea how long it might be before you got paid?"

She laid a hand on his shoulder and said with mock severity, "I'll have you understand, Jess Kingman, I run this store as I see fit!" And at that, a flicker of amusement broke through the somber cast of the man's eyes.

"I guess," he admitted, "you do, at that!"

"Now, don't be missing that stage!" She handed him his hat and turned him toward the door. "When you get there, just ask anyone to show you where the Fergusons

30

live. Dal Chantry and me, we'll take care of things at this end."

"That's right," Chantry told his friend. "You go ahead. By the time the two of you get home, I'll have things fixed up so you'll never know the place."

CHAPTER
FOUR

It was a most informative half hour Dal Chantry spent with Ada Starbuck, helping select the supplies he would need and load them into a buckboard she kept in a stable behind the store. Ada knew the whole story of the Kingmans. She remembered when Jess, with his wife and little girl, first appeared on the Oxbow and started a homestead ranch, only to get into trouble with Luke Blaine who'd used that piece of open range for so long he couldn't see it going under another man's title. She could recall a quarrel over a fence Jess Kingman put up along his boundary; and then there was the talk that began to be heard about stolen beef, with Blaine and his foreman — a man named Garrett — insisting on laying the blame at their unwelcome neighbor's door.

Ada had thought then, and still did, that Jess Kingman simply wasn't the man to have done such things — not even when a posseman was killed trying to arrest him, nor when Ford Garrett went on the witness stand to swear he'd actually seen Kingman working with a bunch of tough hill riders, running off Broken Arrow cattle. There had never been any trace of those other riders. There'd been nothing at all to back

Garrett's accusations, except for some confused and half-obliterated horseshoe prints, and Jess Kingman's failure to produce an alibi.

"But nothing can be done about it now," Ada finished, abruptly switching the subject. "What of yourself, Dal Chantry? Tell me something about your folks."

The young fellow shrugged. "That won't take long. My ma was a laundress at an army post in Utah. Pa was a sergeant. I never did know *him* — the Araphoes got him first. Ma died of consumption when I was eight."

Ada Starbuck was listening, with a look of sympathy he somehow believed must be sincere. "And you've been on your own ever since?"

"Sure. There was a farmer adopted me once. That's what he called it; actually all he wanted was somebody to do his dirty work, and use his fists on when he got drunk. Last time he tried it I laid his scalp open with a singletree and got the hell out of there."

"You killed him?" the woman exclaimed sharply.

He shook his head. "When I heard he was still alive, I come near going back to finish the job . . . I was thirteen, then. Since, I've knocked around over a lot of territory, doing whatever I could to pick up a dime. Swamped for a jerkline outfit. Worked in stables, helped a blacksmith. Punched cows when anyone would let me."

Under her level, searching regard he held back a few details he might have been tempted to tell, just to see if they would shock her — such as how he'd got his first set of spurs by stealing them off a drunk in the alley behind a Kansas trailtown saloon. Yet, somehow, he didn't feel that this woman could be so easily shocked. Ada Starbuck's brown eyes had a way of seeming to look into him, beneath the surface, and she was familiar enough with the rough edges of life that she could take almost anything in stride.

She said now, "What put you in Deer Lodge?"

"I robbed an express office," he said, looking at her squarely; her expression never altered by a shade, so he told her the rest: "It was over at Miles City. I was broke and hungry — as usual, with me. I ran into a couple of crooks named Brice and Jennings, who promised to cut me in for a share if I'd act as lookout and watch the horses. Everything went wrong. They bungled the job, but I was the one the law gathered in. The judge said he was being lenient, on account of me being hardly but a kid." Chantry's mouth twisted hard. "Lenient! He gave me five years. I'd served four of them, when I got my pardon." He added, "I guess that brings you up to date."

"And how old are you now, Dal?"

"Me? I'm twenty-two . . ."

They got the wagon loaded, Chantry refusing to take anything on tick except the absolute necessities — bags of flour and sugar and coffee, baking powder, canned stuff, a side of bacon. Also a hammer and nails and a tin of kerosene, and a few other items.

He was on the wagon's seat, his and Kingman's saddles in the back with the provisions and their horses tied to the rear, when Ada suddenly said, "Wait just a minute." She went inside and after a moment came out with something in her hands; he saw the shine of metal and a last hesitancy before, deliberately, she offered him the Colt revolver.

"You better take this along," she said. "It's loaded. It belonged to my husband, but I have an idea you and Jess may need it more than I do."

Chantry looked at the weapon, not touching it. "Jess says he'll never use a gun," he told her. "And there's some who'd say it ain't real smart, handing a thing like that to a man with my record."

"There's some wouldn't know a good man if they saw him, either," she replied scornfully. She indicated the load of unpaid-for goods in the buckboard and added with wry humor, "I've got an investment in this outfit, you know. I'll be some easier in my mind if I know you're in a position to defend it!"

"All right," said Chantry, and actually grinned a little. He shoved the Colt behind the waistband of his jeans. There was a new box of shells as well, which he slipped into a pocket of his coat, afterward clucking the team into motion. Ada Starbuck stood alone on the rear loading platform of her store, watching him roll from sight along the alley.

He got out of town without attracting much attention, so far as he could see. The word would soon be out that Jess Kingman was back on the Oxbow, bringing another convict with him, to take over again his abandoned ranch; it remained to be seen what kind of reception the news would get. For the time being he was just as pleased that the few persons who saw the stranger in the wagon, and the two unbranded horses trailing behind, showed no more than idle curiosity.

He rode without hurry, enjoying the sun and the deep sky and the pine smell that drifted down from the heights; there were a lot of things learned this morning that had to be thought over, assimilated, fitted into place. A few clouds hung about the heads of the peaks, as though caught there, and their shadows lay dark upon the timber of lower foothills. Out on the valley's rolling floor, he could see cattle grazing and, at one place, the tawny flag of dust where cowhands were working a bunch, probably getting ready to move it toward summer range. Sunlight flashed briefly from window glass of a distant ranch house; in the grass a meadowlark whistled. Once a whitetail and her fawn leaped across the road ahead and went ghosting into the timber.

It was early afternoon when he turned into the side road, dim and weed grown, that led to Cross K, quitting the main valley trace that pointed toward Luke Blaine's Broken Arrow headquarters. He was on grass now where Cross K beef should be feeding, but wherever he looked he saw only cattle carrying Blaine's brand and that other, strange one — Heart Nine — that Jess Kingman hadn't remembered. He should have thought to ask Ada Starbuck about Heart Nine, but there'd been too many other things that needed asking.

The moment he brought the forsaken Cross K buildings in view, he sighted a clot of five saddled horses standing in the yard.

Chantry felt the sharp, tight knotting in his belly and halted the rig for a moment as he considered this. There was nothing else to see — merely the unmoving, head-drooping broncs waiting there in the sun and silence; but it was enough. To Chantry it meant one thing: The trouble he half expected had beaten him here.

His mouth set hard, and deliberately he put the team in motion again. Approaching, he kept a careful watch for any sign of the owners of those horses and was rewarded, still some distance from the house, when he saw a man come out and, crossing the porch, step down to take one of them by the reins. Suddenly he turned and apparently called a warning. After that he stood waiting as the newcomer tooled his wagon into the weedy yard and brought it to a halt.

Chantry glanced toward the brands on the horses. Four were Broken Arrows; the one whose reins the man was holding carried a Heart Nine. Looking at him Chantry saw a spare-bodied man, well enough dressed, with a contained and shrewd look about his clean-shaven features. He didn't seem to be wearing a gun. But now a second man came striding out onto the porch, and instantly demanded Dal Chantry's attention.

This was a big fellow — big enough that his shaggy head made an unconscious ducking motion as he moved through the doorway. He was wide as well as tall, and his arms below rolled shirtsleeves carried a bunching of corded muscle. He was probably in his late forties, but he looked younger except for a salting gray in his tight, curling mop of black hair. His features were heavy, his brows scowling above deepset eyes. Immediately Chantry saw the gun he wore strapped to one thick leg.

Taking a stance on the porch with boots spread wide and massive shoulders rolled forward, the man looked at Chantry and the wagon — the stuff piled in back, the pair of horses trailing. He said heavily, "Lookin' for somebody?" His voice was big enough to match his frame. The question was an insult, the way he spoke it.

Chantry said, "Where's the men that belong to the rest of these horses?"

The thick shoulders lifted. "Around."

"Then tell them to mount up and get off Cross K property."

"You go to hell!"

Chantry watched the big hands knot tight and then loosen again. The barrel chest swelled to a drawn breath. "I reckon I know you, kid. You're that other jailbird Kingman brought home with him."

"That's right." He swallowed a furtive disappointment. After all, what could he have expected? What reason did he have to think Gwen Macaulay wouldn't ride straight home last night with warning to her uncle of the new arrivals at Cross K, so that Luke Blaine could look after his own interests? "The name," he said, "is Chantry."

"Uh huh." The big man sounded as though he couldn't have been less interested. "Well, Garrett's my handle. You've heard it, I guess."

38

Ford Garrett: so this was the foreman of Broken Arrow. Now another pair of men came drifting into view around a corner of the house, as though drawn by the sound of their talk. Cowhands by the look of them, and of little consequence — but they were armed.

That still left one to be accounted for, and now Chantry saw him, too.

He stepped through the doorway behind the foreman, but he came so quietly by contrast with Garrett's porch-shaking tromp that Chantry scarcely noticed him until, suddenly, he was there at the edge of the roof shadow. His voice as he spoke seemed like little more than a whisper, after Garrett's booming shout. "You're taking up valuable time, boy."

Chantry looked at the speaker and recognized him for what he was. It didn't take the careful hang of his holstered gun to brand him. The eyes alone — black, hard, penetrating — were enough. Dal Chantry knew a professional when he saw one.

He was past being heedful of danger. He looked at the foreman as, scornfully, he said, "Is this what Broken Arrow has on its payroll, Garrett? Hired guns?"

A mocking grin suddenly spread Garrett's lips. "Sometimes a gun like Ed Varner's comes in handy," he admitted. "Like when some tough punk tries to make trouble!" The grin hardened. "Let me set you straight, kid: this ain't Cross K. As of today, it's a Broken Arrow line camp. We been intending to take it over — it ain't much, but we need one about here and it'll serve. And now you turn that rig and get the hell out of here!"

"No!" shouted Chantry.

All at once he was standing, with one boot on the iron rim of the forward wheel. The gunman, Ed Varner, stiffened. He dropped a hand upon the polished butt of his waist gun as he said sharply, "Don't get off that wagon!"

Dal Chantry leaped.

He simply catapulted himself off the rim of that wheel, and across the narrow distance separating him from the porch. Ed Varner reacted swiftly, his gun sliding from holster in a blur of light; but Chantry's lunge drove into the gunman and the elbow of Varner's lifting arm struck a porch prop.

The gun bounced out of his fingers, going end for end. It struck the hub of the wagon's wheel and spun into the weeds. Varner, with Chantry on top of him, twisted around the post and nearly went down in a tangle of the floorboards. Dal Chantry, even as he leaped, was tearing at the gun behind his own waistband and he ripped it free now. His boots slipped on the edge of the porch, found purchase. He slammed the gunman back against the post and held him there while the gun Ada Starbuck had given him rose and chopped down, hard. Varner's hat took some of the force of the blow; it tumbled off his head and the gunman went suddenly limp.

Chantry let him go. As the man doubled forward and took a helpless dive off the edge of the porch, he swung about and let the gun drop level, to menace the others. "The next one," he cried harshly, "I shoot!"

They stood hardly breathing, gaping at the muzzle of the gun and at the fury in the eyes above it. Chantry had lost his own hat, and black hair had tumbled in wings to frame either side of his pale and sweat-glistening face. He was daring, even inviting, a challenging move and they clearly knew it. Of them all, only the Heart Nine man seemed not to be startled or perturbed; he stood there calmly enough, looking at the young fellow and his gun with an expression that seemed to hold only a cool interest.

Dal Chantry had recovered a little, now, from his blind and reckless anger. He told them, "The lot of you are trespassing on deeded land! I'd have every legal right to do more than merely kick you off." He was still having trouble with his breathing as he lifted the barrel of the gun, and his thumb curled about the hammerspur. "Now, start moving. You've got maybe two seconds!"

One of the punchers, a skinny, red-faced man, asked hesitantly, "What about our stuff? In the house?"

"Leave it!" Chantry snapped. "Tell Luke Blaine if he'll send a man over tomorrow — *one* man, no more than that — I'll let him pick it up." He added, with a nod toward the gunman lying facedown in the dead weeds, "But that you can take with you!"

The Broken Arrow hands looked at their foreman. Ford Garrett was holding himself in with an act of will; there was pure outrage in the look he put on this stranger who, at scarcely half his years, had bested him and three of his crew. He shuddered through all his big frame now, and flung a tight and angry order at his men: "Put Varner on his horse!"

They moved quickly enough, once the order was given. Ed Varner was picked off the ground and carried, head limp and arms swaying, to his mount and slung belly down across the saddle. The skinny one returned for the gunman's hat and, as he got it, saw Varner's gun lying in the weeds. Chantry said quietly, "No."

"Let it alone, Slim," the foreman grunted. Slim trotted willingly enough back to his horse and swung astride, taking the reins of Varner's mount. The punchers waited there in the yard then, with Garrett's horse ready for him. But the foreman wasn't yet ready to go. He glowered at the man with the gun, beneath the shaggy tangle of his brows.

He said, "Because you're nothing but a young punk, you got away with it this time; don't expect such luck to last. There's no place for you and that other jailbird on the Oxbow. You better believe it!"

Chantry didn't answer because he didn't trust himself. Garrett, having voiced his warning, turned abruptly and dropping off the porch strode heavily out to his waiting horse. It was a big brute of an animal, a deep-barreled gelding built to carry the foreman's bulk. The saddle creaked under him as he dragged it to one side, putting his weight into the stirrup; he swung a solid leg over and settled into place.

Dal Chantry realized he should have disarmed the Broken Arrow men — in his reckless rage, he simply hadn't thought of it. But, apparently, none of them felt inclined to try a move; Chantry's tension eased as he saw Ford Garrett yank the gelding's head around and slap the spurs to it. The animal leaped ahead and settled into a long gait. The two punchers followed quickly and they went out of sight that way, Ed Varner's dangling arms and legs swinging to the rhythm of the horses.

Drawing a breath, Chantry turned to the Heart Nine man. "And what about you?" he demanded.

The man, who had watched all this without speaking a word, quickly shook his head. He was about medium tall, in jeans and boots and a corduroy jacket with elbows reinforced by leather patches. Chantry saw now that he had blue eyes of a startling paleness, rather like chips of glass. He said, "I'm not here to make trouble. I only dropped by out of curiosity — in fact, to see what Blaine's men were doing where they had no business. You can put the gun away."

But Chantry took his own time deciding about that, wondering if there could be a weapon strapped on beneath that corduroy jacket. He said roughly, "You're not a friend of Ford Garrett's?"

"I get along with him. I try to get along with all my neighbors."

Chantry eyed the brand on the horse. "Heart Nine, huh?"

"My outfit," the man said, and nodded vaguely westward, toward the lift of rock and timber that edged the valley. "Over toward the hills. Steve Roman's the name," he added.

He might have been a rather handsome fellow once, actually, but now encroaching middle age — or was it liquor? — was beginning to work on him, loosening the jowls, blurring the sharp outlines, etching the cheeks with a tiny pattern of broken blood vessels. Chantry couldn't really say just what it was about the man that gave him a strong, repellent sense of physical uncleanness.

Nevertheless, he lowered the gun; at once Steve Roman relaxed his cautious alertness and fetched out a box of readymade cigarettes from a pocket of his coat and selected one. He pushed the flat-crowned hat back from his forehead, revealing a receding hairline. Chantry said, "You must be new around here, since Jess Kingman's time. He said he couldn't remember the brand."

"He wouldn't." Roman examined the cigarette, turning it in lean and spatulate fingers. "But I dare say he'll remember me, though not as a rancher. No — hardly!" That seemed to strike him as amusing, because he laughed a little over it; but the laugh failed to warm his pale eyes in the slightest. "Oh, life holds many changes, my young friend, as I'm sure you've learned before this. It's the one thing I can guarantee you'll continue to learn as you get older. *If* you get older, that is," he added. "Which I don't guarantee — not if that was the way you treat men like Garrett and Ed Varner!"

Dal Chantry said nothing to that, and the other shoved his cigarette between flat lips. He had dug up a kitchen match; he popped it on a thumbnail and used it to get the cigarette to burning. He turned and found the stirrup of his waiting horse, stepped easily into the saddle.

"Just a minute!"

The pale eyes stared at him and Chantry went on, in the same uncompromising tone. "I might as well say this to you now: you've got cattle on Jess Kingman's grass. Naturally, you'll see about moving them off."

Steve Roman met the challenging look without any expression whatever. Then: "Naturally," he said, and backing his horse clear of the wagon he left there at an easy, reaching canter.

Dal Chantry, watching him out of sight, was still fighting to settle the tensions of that encounter with Broken Arrow. It took him some moments to realize that, concerning this Steve Roman, he'd managed to learn precisely nothing at all.

CHAPTER
FIVE

Arrival time for the weekly stage, southbound, from Hermit Flat was roughly in the area of noon, and Chantry got to town well before then so as to be sure of meeting it. He had no certain knowledge that Kingman and his girl would be on that particular coach, but that had been the final word, and he could see no reason why Millie Kingman's affairs in Hermit Flat couldn't have been settled in time. In the random haphazard pattern of his own life there had been few strings or hindrances. As the saying had it, when you wanted to move on all you had to do was throw water on the fire and call the dogs . . .

It was a still noontime, and in Oxbow a woodsmoke tang of dinner fires mingled with the scent of pines. He looked first for a public corral, where there were usually animals and rigs to be hired. Here he arranged to rent a horse and single-seated buggy for use that afternoon, though he had to argue a while before he reached a price he could afford. Of course he could likely have had the free loan of Ada Starbuck's team and rig, but somehow it seemed unfitting for Millie Kingman to make her return home in an old wagon without springs, and one axle bent out of true.

So, at least, it seemed to Dal Chantry — who had never had a home.

It was still too early for stage time, so he left his horse at the corral and went along the sun-shimmering street on foot, toward a dismal looking stone building whose small, barred windows had caused at first sight an unpleasant reaction in him — until he remembered that he was a free man now, unbeholden to any symbol of the law, and with no need to dread the sight of a jail. Today, he figured, he had honest business there. When he turned the knob of the office door it failed to open. He tried again, decided it was locked. As he stood there, a voice he didn't know spoke his name.

"If you're looking for the deputy sheriff, Chantry, you won't find him."

He looked around. A man had just emerged from a diner next door. He returned Dal Chantry's look with a stare that was definitely a challenge, and Chantry's own eyes narrowed — the man knew his name, yet he was not anyone Chantry had ever met.

The stranger had the stamp of a prosperous cattleman, from fawn-colored Stetson to California pants tucked into bench-made boots. A shock of white hair showed below his hatbrim. Years of sun and weather had darkened his skin but not roughened it, and the white of the hair and the heavy moustache stood out sharply against the smooth brown face. There was an intensity about the man, an impatience that could express itself as ruthlessness where his intentions were thwarted.

He said, continuing his previous statement, "I sent Irv Wallace to the county seat on business. I wouldn't look for him back till tomorrow at the earliest."

So this was a man who could use the local representative of the sheriff's office as his personal errand boy. Any remaining question Chantry might have about him was answered when, in the next moment, the diner's screen door whined open and Ford Garrett came out, sucking at a toothpick. Seeing Chantry, the Broken Arrow foreman scowled and at once stepped up beside the solid figure of the cowman. He said roughly, "That's him, Luke. That's the fellow."

Luke Blaine nodded. "I judged as much."

"And you're Blaine?" Dal Chantry said.

The cowman nodded again. His eyes raked the stranger, the whole shabby length of him. He plainly noted the lack of a holster or weapon. Blaine was unarmed, himself; but then, he didn't need to wear a gun because he had his foreman for that. Ford Garrett, standing hipshot beside his employer, let his fingers drum silently on the leather of the holster strapped to his leg. The toothpick wheeled between his lips as he chewed on it, while his eyes watched Chantry with an expression of pure malevolence.

Luke Blaine said, "I been curious as to the kind of nerve it would take to jump four of my men and send them all packing. A real tough boy, I'd thought to hear it. But you don't look much more than a kid!"

Garrett spat out the toothpick, his face hardening. "Damn it, Luke, I already told you how it was. He ain't tough — he just don't have good sense, or he'd never have tried what he done!"

The white-haired rancher never glanced at his foreman.

"Which is it, boy?" he demanded. "Are you tough — or just stupid?"

Chantry countered: "What are you wondering? Whether it's safe to risk sending your men to try and take Cross K back? Well, I'll let you have something else to wonder about; I'll pass on to you what I was going to tell the deputy."

"Yes?" Blaine waited.

Chantry's reckless anger was heating up as he saw the insolence in this man. "It was a message for you — and for Steve Roman, and any other that's been running cattle on Jess Kingman's range. You've all had free grazing privileges on deeded land, and for a damn long time. Now I'm serving notice that that land's being posted. You've got one week to move your cattle off. If not they'll be seized and impounded, to help pay for some of the grass they've been eating."

He had laid down his ultimatum and he waited to see its effect. Luke Blaine's chin lifted a trifle, and Ford Garrett stiffened out of his negligent slouch. For a long moment the three of them stood on the splintered, weathered boards of the sidewalk with all the normal sounds of noonday around them. It was Blaine who finally spoke.

"You were going to tell Deputy Wallace that, were you?"

Chantry nodded stiffly. "I was . . . I am!"

Garrett exploded. "By God, you and Kingman will pay hell making it stick! Stinking jailbirds! Who gives a damn for anything you want?"

The nails of Dal Chantry's fists were grinding into his palms suddenly; his chest swelled with the old, familiar ache as his controls slipped. "Unstrap that gun," he said between his teeth. "If you've got the nerve!"

He saw the foreman's face whipped white by the lash of his words, and then angry red seeped into its planes and Ford Garrett was fumbling at the buckle of his gunbelt, yanking savagely at the leather tongue to disengage and free it. Luke Blaine had to speak twice, sharply, before his words could penetrate.

"Stop it! You know I won't have my crew brawling on the town streets! As for you, boy . . ." Sharp eyes, under the white thickets of his brows, bored into Chantry. "You, and that cow thief, had just better watch your steps. Because nobody around here is going to let you get away with anything!"

All kinds of furious answers tumbled over one another on Chantry's tongue. What foolish blunder he might have committed next, he was fortunately never to know, for suddenly he became aware of a growing sound that penetrated through the red fog of his anger. He swung away, and saw the stagecoach pouring up the street in a boil of dust and an uproar of pounding hooves, with rumbling wheels and groaning timbers and shaking harness chains.

The coach hit town with the driver yelling at his teams and a mongrel dog in its wake. At his glimpse of

Jess Kingman's familiar shape in a window as the stage rolled by, Dal Chantry forced himself to settle. He allowed himself one last, cold regard for the Broken Arrow men. Then, deliberately, he turned his back and walked away from them, past the jail to the log station where the big coach was even now rocking to a halt, brake shoes smoking.

Saffron-colored dust lifted and settled. The driver wrapped his reins to the ironwork of the dash and began to climb down, but Jess Kingman opened the door himself, not waiting. As he emerged from the coach, Chantry had a momentary feeling that he was really looking at his friend, clearly, for the first time, and seeing just how wasted and frail he actually was. He thought, *Why, he's an old man! An old man, at scarcely fifty!* Prison had done it — prison and the men who had sent him there.

Kingman reached up a hand and, as Chantry neared, was just helping a girl in a gray traveling dress out of the coach. Now he caught sight of his partner and motioned to him; pride swelled his voice as he said, "Here she is, Dal. This is Millie . . ."

Chantry had no idea of what he had expected Kingman's daughter to be. His first impression was of smallness and fragility, and of great, soft eyes raised timidly to his. The eyes were blue, rather like her father's; there the resemblance ended. Her hair was, dark as a crow's wing, her face heartshaped and delicately modeled and her mouth was that of someone vulnerable to hurt. A lovely girl, altogether, but one who roused troubled feelings that she should be protected.

She was something utterly foreign to Dal Chantry's rough existence, and he was suddenly overwhelmed with awkwardness. He said, "How do?" gruffly, and pushed out a big, hard-calloused hand.

Millie Kingman's eyes held his own; she bobbed her head and slipped a small hand into his grasp. "I'm very well, thank you," she said, shyly formal. And then, with what must have been an impulsive effort, she added, "I'm so glad to know you. After all Papa's letters — I feel almost as though I do, already!"

"Yes, ma'am. Reckon I feel the same."

"Didn't I tell you she was something special, boy?" Jess Kingman still held to his daughter's arm, almost as though afraid something might happen to take her away again, and out of his life. "Nobody could ever really know! Why, she's her mother all over again. They couldn't be more alike . . ."

And then a change came over Jess Kingman, something that stiffened him as his blue eyes, widening, shifted to a point beyond Dal Chantry. The latter saw his face drain of color, then he, too, looked around at Luke Blaine and his foreman.

For a moment, everything was forgotten — the street sounds, the activity about the stagecoach, where another pair of passengers was alighting while the station agent helped the driver unload freight from the top of the coach. As Dal Chantry watched his friend face these ancient enemies, the meeting seemed to him to hold the tension of a cocked gun.

Luke Blaine was the first to speak. "So it *is* you, Kingman!" His cold stare ranged the wasted frame of the smaller man. "The years have changed you."

"In twelve years, you've changed some yourself." Kingman spoke quietly enough, but one could have guessed he was making the comparison between the healthy, prosperous look of the Broken Arrow rancher, and his own sorry prison pallor. Anyone would have said Kingman was considerably the older, yet in point of fact Chantry knew that Blaine had more than a decade on him.

Now Blaine looked at Millie Kingman, who was watching all this with a seeming lack of comprehension — probably she did not remember these men, hadn't guessed at their identity. Blaine said gruffly, "And this is the girl? Somehow I'd lost sight that she existed — only a child then, as I remember. I see she's growed up to look like her mother." He turned again to Jess. "Do I understand Miz Kingman has passed on?"

He spoke respectfully enough, but the other answered with biting crispness: "That's something we won't discuss, Luke! Long as we have to live on the same range, I may try to forgive what was done to me. But what happened to her — never!"

A faint stain of color crept into the other's cheeks; his white tangle of brows pinched down. Beside him, Ford Garrett's full lips twisted in a disdainful sneer. "So now he's talking about forgiving people! Hell, Luke! You'd think it was somebody other than him was convicted of cow stealin' and manslaughter!"

Dal Chantry couldn't hold himself back. "Better tell him to shut his yap, Blaine," he warned. "Or somebody's apt to shut it for him!"

Concern for his friend's wild temper probably helped Jess Kingman control his own. He drew a quick breath, speaking before the angry Garrett could frame an answer. "We don't need that sort of talk, Dal. We're not here to make trouble, unless it's pushed onto us."

Chantry's challenging stare continued to hold the foreman. "They've started the pushing! When I got back to the ranch the day you left, Garrett and a tough crew were already trying to move in."

"That wasn't on my orders," Luke Blaine put in quickly. "Ford simply wanted to find out what you'd do about it."

"Well, he found out!" snapped Chantry. Then he added, "I've just got through telling the both of them, Jess: any beef doesn't get moved off Cross K within the week is gonna be impounded."

He drew a startled, worried glance from Kingman; then the older man sighed, and slowly nodded. "That was pretty blunt. But, just so they understand . . ."

"Then you go along with this?" Luke Blaine demanded, scowling. "You back him up?"

Jess Kingman looked suddenly very tired, as he answered. "I have to go along. The boy was in his rights. It's our grass."

"Maybe," Blaine grunted. "And maybe not — we'll have to see." Letting that dangle, he straightened his shoulders, his manner indicating the talk was finished. "I don't know what you expected, Kingman — but you certainly couldn't think anyone would be pleased to have you back. Especially when you bring trouble like this with you!" His scowl indicated Chantry.

Stiffly, then, he touched hatbrim to Millie Kingman. "Good day, miss!" His elbow gave Ford Garrett a nudge that prodded the tough foreman out of his belligerent stance. They turned, shouldering past a knot of curious onlookers, and tramped away together along the plank sidewalk — two big men, arrogant in the knowledge of their ranking as owner and straw boss of the Oxbow's biggest cattle spread.

A look from Chantry raked the bystanders, and as one man they seemed to become aware of business to take them elsewhere. As they drifted off he turned back, scowling. "Reckon I only made things worse than they was with that pair," he admitted gruffly. "Sorry." He looked at Millie Kingman. "Anyhow," he added wryly, "welcome home!"

Her eyes appeared darker and larger than ever against the pallor of her face. Plainly, she'd been terrified by the explosive violence of that scene, and she even drew back a little from Dal Chantry now — perhaps she saw the wildness still reflected in his face. The thought helped to sober him, and settle his raw temper. Jess Kingman, unnoticing, sighed and shook his head.

"I'm sorry that meeting had to happen," he said, "today of all days! I've always known it would be bad; but at least it's behind us. Let's go home."

"I've rented a rig," Dal Chantry said. "But right now it's meal time, and I think Ada Starbuck's planning dinner for us in case we stop by."

"Oh, could we?" Millie quickly exclaimed, as eager as a child. "She's always been such a good friend."

"Of course," Jess Kingman said, and smiled. "I'll fetch your things . . ."

Left alone with the girl for a moment, Dal Chantry saw how she put a long, searching look around her. "Town seem familiar?" he asked.

"I — think so." But she seemed unsure. "I was so very young when we left. There isn't much I do remember, from all those years ago. And so much I don't want to remember . . ."

Kingman was back, carrying a carpetbag; there would also be a small trunk to pick up later, when they had the rig and team. Chantry took the carpetbag and with the girl between them they walked away, unheedful of curious, staring eyes. When they turned off Main in the direction of Starbuck's, they could see Ada Starbuck already waiting on the stoop — her smile beaming, her arms waiting to take Millie into a motherly embrace.

56

CHAPTER
SIX

Irv Wallace, sheriff's representative in the Oxbow district, returned from the county seat with information that had to be passed on immediately to Luke Blaine; fortunately Blaine was in town that day on some business of his own and the deputy was spared a further ride to Broken Arrow. Shortly after he got the jail office opened and was airing out the stale, slop jar odors from the cell block, Blaine joined him. Hat on knee and an expensive cigar rolling between his meaty lips, the cattleman sat on the other side of the desk and listened to the report Wallace had brought him.

"It's all legal and on the books, Mr. Blaine." Wallace was a small man, sandy-haired and jowly, with some disease of the eyelids that made him blink compulsively when he was nervous. The displeasure he saw in the cowman's face made his whole face work as he squinted. "I done what I could. I searched the tax records, clear on back; I talked the whole business over with the sheriff, and the district attorney."

"And there's nothing?"

"Nothing. Kingman's title is clear; every assessment against his land has always been paid. We're left no loophole at all."

Blaine scowled at the hands that were folded across his paunch; he rubbed his thumbs together and worked blue clouds of smoke from the cigar to hang before his face. "Hell!" he muttered explosively. The barrel chair creaked as he shifted his solid weight. "Who ever would have thought it? It never once occurred to me but what title to that section must have reverted to the county years ago . . . And so there's no legal way to get rid of those convicts? Is that what it comes to?"

"Afraid not, Mr. Blaine. Nobody give me any encouragement, none at all."

"Uh huh." Luke Blaine plucked the half-smoked cigar from his mouth, looked at it, and with an angry gesture flung it into the bucket of slops beside the jail desk. "Well, then that's that. Looks like I'll have to find other ways."

He swung to his feet. Wallace, looking up at him, fluttered nervous fingertips on the scarred desktop. He blinked furiously as he tried for words. "I hope you'll be — uh — discreet," he managed, and then his sagging jowls colored to the look the rancher gave him.

"Are you reminding me to stay within the law?" Luke Blaine snapped. "By God, I could resent that, Irv! Remember, you're talking to me — not that cheap crook Kingman!"

Irv Wallace swallowed. "Sorry, I didn't mean —"

"A man who's big enough," Blaine continued, overriding him, "don't break the law — he uses it. In all the years getting where I am today, I defy anyone to prove one illegal move against me. I'm proud of that record, and don't you forget it!"

Overcome, the deputy could only nod wordlessly. And Blaine pulled on his expensive, fawn-colored Stetson, and tramped outside to his waiting horse.

Luke Blaine was deep in his own thoughts. When, mounted, he met Ada Starbuck passing along the boardwalk he scarcely saw her; next moment, though, he was reining in and pulling the big bay horse around in a tight circle. "Ada!" he said.

She turned, her head under its beaded bonnet tilting to one side as she looked up at him. She said nothing, merely waiting. Blaine kneed his horse closer and leaned from the saddle, a forearm resting on his knee as his gloved hand toyed with the rein ends. He said without preliminary, "I understand you're being pretty generous about giving credit, these days, out of that store of yours."

Her manner was completely reserved, as impersonal as his own. "Yes?"

"I hear you're carrying that outfit at Cross K on the books — for anything they should happen to want. Is that good business?"

Her mouth tightened; her head tilted a little more. "You so concerned about me, Luke? Maybe I should be flattered."

"I'm simply wondering," he replied, his voice roughening, "why a pair of jailbirds deserve special treatment, as against a customer who's given you a lot of trade, over a good many years — and never asked a single favor."

"Why, Luke," she corrected him calmly, "you don't ask — you take! I'm yet to see the day when you couldn't pay cash, but, now, if you mean you'd like to open an account —"

"Let's quit beating around the bush!" He straightened abruptly, throwing the words down at the woman from his commanding height in the saddle. "I won't have such neighbors, and I won't have them encouraged! If you prefer their business to mine, I can always start having my supplies hauled directly from the railhead. Would you like that?"

Ada Starbuck's face lost some of its color; her matronly bosom swelled beneath its shawl as she caught her breath. But her voice was steady enough.

"You know I wouldn't like it! Broken Arrow's trade supports my business, the same as it does nine-tenths of the people in this town. But I won't turn my back on old friends. Nor will I be blackmailed. So, you go right ahead — if you can do such a low, hound dog sort of thing! Especially to a poor widow woman!"

Her words rang in the quiet street. Luke Blaine's thick white moustache bristled and his face grew red. He retreated into bluster.

"I've said my say," he told her, and lifted the reins. "Jess Kingman is a thief and a killer. I got rid of him once, and if he don't watch his step I'll do it again. And when I do, don't think I won't remember who his friends were!" And he clapped a heel to the bay's flank and rode away, ramrod-straight in the saddle, a man not given to bending.

He headed for Broken Arrow in a savage mood, knowing he had no choice but to give Ford Garrett his orders, and start his cattle moving off Cross K grass.

60

It was all very puzzling. The sign was clear enough — a dozen or twenty head of cattle, moving out of a belt of timber at the lower end of this meadow, had milled briefly about the margin of a seep spring before they vanished into a timbered draw pointing toward the upward folds of the hills. To Jess Kingman, there was no doubt they had been driven; there was no reason for cattle moving on their own to leave good grass and water, once they'd found it, for the tougher country higher up. And if cow sense wasn't enough to convince him, there was the clear sign in the trampled mud at the spring's edge: shod horses, a pair of them, the prints distinct and definite.

Since the sign was fairly recent — not older than yesterday — his first angry thought was that Broken Arrow, or some other outfit, was showing further defiance and contempt for his rights to his own range by continuing to work it, and move stock around on it, as though it were free grass open to anyone. But then this line of reasoning was bothered by a nagging doubt. For what sense could there be in deliberately pushing cattle into that particular upcountry? Nothing there in the way of feed and water; nothing but timber and rock and increasingly rough going, and no place to go unless you were determined to push through the hills to the other side.

Trying to make sense of it, he sat and stared at nothing for a moment as his sorrel horse moved restlessly under him, and a dragonfly stitched an iridescent pattern in the still, warm air above the spring. He pulled off his hat and ran a hand across his thinning hair — and then his head jerked about and he stared, as a clot of riders broke from the lower pines and came directly toward him across the grass. He replaced the hat, dropped his hand to the saddle-horn.

There were five of them, and the one in the lead was an old enemy, Ford Garrett. Kingman tensed and then forced his nerves to loosen; he had only himself to blame that he'd been caught alone here. He had wanted to look over this ranch of his again and knowing the memories it would awaken he'd asked Millie and Dal to stay behind. And so here he was — alone.

They came steadily on, hooves whispering in wire grass, and fanning out a little. The rest halted but Garrett came right ahead, crowding Kingman and only pulling rein, their knees almost touching, when he saw the latter meant to stand his ground. A dangerous scowl marked the foreman's broad face. "All right, Kingman," he said harshly, and he nodded toward the tracks of the missing cattle. "You think you're doing something clever? Where are they?"

Jess Kingman faced him squarely, not letting himself show any evidence of fear. "I can see the sign," he answered coldly. "I just now found it. That's all I know."

The flat lips lifted in a sneer. "You know nothing about seventeen head of prime Broken Arrow stock, I guess. You're back less than a week and already it's starting — but I guess you and that other jailbird didn't have nothing to do with running them off!"

"It's the truth," Kingman insisted doggedly. "Just as it was twelve years ago!"

"Oh, sure!" Garrett's look was almost pitying. "You never will get smart, will you? Do you know what Luke Blaine told us this morning? That we were to come and gather his stuff and start moving it back off this grass you say is yours. That's right!" He nodded with a grin, as he saw Kingman's astonished expression. "You came that close to pulling your bluff and making it stick — and then you had to go and overplay your hand. Wait till Luke hears. His orders will change fast enough. He ain't gonna let you get away with *this!*"

Kingman's chest swelled, as years of repressed anger threatened to burst in futile violence. But long discipline came to his aid and his voice when he allowed himself to speak was level enough. "You worked your frame once before. I suppose you might think you can do it again."

At that, Garrett's face turned hard. He half turned to the other men. "You hear him?" he said loudly. "The fellow's still talking frame-up!"

Jess Kingman looked at the Broken Arrow riders, and the stares they returned were completely cold, completely unfriendly. They were strangers, of course — the normal turnover of hands on a cow country spread would assure that — but they plainly accepted the official story of the events of a dozen years ago; their faces held a closed and hostile condemnation that was all too familiar. There was bitterness in him as he turned back to their leader.

63

He said as quietly as he could, "You know as well as I do that I never touched a head of Luke Blaine's stock — or anyone else's. You've known it all these years. Has it ever bothered your sleep any, knowing it?"

The warning flags were out, in Garrett's furious scowl. "What do you think you're trying to make me say?"

"Come off it, Ford," Jess Kingman said. "You're not on the witness stand, you know. There's no need for you to lie, now . . ."

He had prodded a shade too hard — or perhaps there actually was some buried quirk of conscience that all at once broke through the foreman's controls. Rage flamed in his eyes, set his voice to trembling. "Shut up!" he cried. "*Shut up!*" Suddenly his big hand was fumbling at the holster on his belt, and rising with a Colt revolver engulfed in it. Alarm spread through Jess Kingman. Almost without thinking he flung an arm across the space between their saddles; his fingers groped and closed on the barrel of the gun. It was the wrong thing to do. Garrett seemed to go berserk. The heavy face — sweating now — twisted into no recognizable pattern. With a shout of rage he jerked back and the weapon roared beneath both their hands.

Jess Kingman felt a smashing blow. Reeling, he groped for the saddlehorn, but even as his fingers closed upon it they were already growing numb and without sensation. Through glazing eyes he stared at Ford Garrett's sweaty face. Then the world lost light and substance. The echoes of the shot were still pulsing in his ears when he sank swiftly into blackness.

The barn at Cross K was well built and solidly framed, as only a cow country barn could be. Despite years of neglect it stood as square and firm as the day it was built. A number of its roof shakes had been stripped away by wind and weather, and Dal Chantry had rived out new ones and was up on a ladder giving an hour to the job of patching and replacing. He had a good view, from there, along the river bottom. When he sighted a pair of riders approaching he immediately gave them a part of his attention, putting an occasional glance on them as they came slowly nearer.

Presently they were close enough to take on definite shape, and then it was that Chantry thought he recognized one of the horses — a big chestnut — while its rider was still too far away to identify. Instantly alert, he finished with the shingle he was placing, deliberately hammering home the last nail. After that he came down the ladder, laid his tools aside, and started for the house. He went without haste, but his timing was such that he had stepped up onto the porch and placed a shoulder against a roof prop moments before the horsemen jingled into the dooryard.

He had guessed right about the chestnut. The rider was Steve Roman, and both horses wore his Heart Nine brand. His companion was a nondescript fellow, evidently a cowhand, whose enormous cascade of moustache seemed weight enough to bow his head forward and give his eyes their sagging droop, like a bloodhound's. The eyes were too close together, and this stirred a deep-seated prejudice in Chantry.

He dismissed him, and looked at Roman, remembering Jess Kingman's astonished reaction when Dal Chantry had asked what he knew about the man: "Steve Roman? That tinhorn! I had no idea he'd still be around; thought he'd have drifted long ago. Or more likely, got himself shot over one of those poker tables at the Red Dog — that's how his breed usually ends up."

"Not Roman. He may have been a tinhorn gambler when you knew him twelve years ago. Now he's a rancher."

"I'll have to see that for myself . . ."

Now that he knew the man's history, it seemed to Dal Chantry he could see undefinable traces of his origin. It was in the way he bore himself, and in the expressionless gambler's facade — the pale stare that was all surface, and showed nothing of depth. Roman thumbed the hat back from his receding hairline and cast an appraising glance around the ranch headquarters, noting the porch, whose rotten stringers Chantry had replaced, and the new glass in the windows. He said pleasantly, "Quite an improvement, in a few days. You're making the place look almost lived in."

When the young fellow made no answer, Steve Roman went on. "Kingman's not around? Being neighbors and old acquaintances, I thought I should pay my respects."

Chantry made no effort to hide his dislike of the man. "Looks like you'd have to try again."

"That's all right. There's plenty of time," the man said with a shrug. He added dryly, "Or we can hope so at least!" He lifted the reins. "Just tell your partner that —" His words broke off and his pale stare traveled beyond Chantry, to the open door of the house. Dal Chantry knew before he turned that it would be Millie Kingman who, hearing voices in the yard, had stepped to the doorway for a look.

She had been hanging window curtains. She wore an apron over her sunny yellow house dress, and her hair was pinned up out of the way; she looked an odd combination of mature woman and child as she stood there with her large, dark eyes fastened on the rider of the chestnut. Turning back, Chantry thought for a moment he actually surprised some trace of emotion on the ex-gambler's face — though what emotion it was, he could scarcely say.

For a long minute Steve Roman stared at the girl, then, slowly, put up a hand and lifted his hat to her. "Is this really Miss Kingman?" he exclaimed. "It never occurred to me — !"

Vaguely irritated, Dal Chantry cut him off. "I'll tell Jess you came by, Roman."

The pale eyes switched back to him. Steve Roman appeared to accept his dismissal. Replacing the hat, he took up the reins in strong, lean fingers. "No question about it," he murmured, his eyes once more on the girl in the doorway. "You'll be seeing me again!" Apparently untroubled that she hadn't said a word in reply, he turned his horse, and the puncher with the moustache fell in beside him. Dal Chantry, scowling, watched them ride away, continuing south along the road that led to Oxbow.

He straightened from his lean against the roofpost and turned, starting to say something which he left unspoken when he saw the look on Millie's face. It was a look of distress and vague alarm, like that of someone starting from a bad dream, and it brought him hastily to her side. "Why, what is it?"

Her eyes, following the disappearing riders, seemed to return to him as from a long way off. "That man!" she exclaimed, in a tone of pure revulsion. "I — I don't think I like him!"

Disturbed, Chantry could only shrug. "According to your pa he ain't much, for a fact — a tinhorn gambler, turned respectable. I seen the way he was looking at you," he added sourly. "A man at least twice your age! Well, don't let it bother you. If he comes around and you don't like it — we'll get rid of him, fast enough!"

But she was still plainly troubled, though she gave him a brief smile as she turned back into the house. Chantry stood for a long couple of minutes, scowling after the pair who had already vanished into the sunsmear on the Valley bottom. After that, still wondering a little at Millie's strange reaction, he returned to his work.

Having finished one side of the roof, he carried the long homemade ladder around and propped it against the opposite wall of the barn. He went to fetch his hammer and box of nails and another armload of shingles. About to climb the ladder, he heard the ragged, unrhythmic sound of nearing hooves. He turned and for a moment froze, unmoving.

The sorrel horse, making its lagging and erratic way toward him, was an animal he knew well. The rider who clung drunkenly and brokenly to the saddle was Jess Kingman.

CHAPTER
SEVEN

Something under a week had seen a lot of changes in the Cross K ranch house, thanks partly to Ada Starbuck who'd gone far out of her way in helping prepare for Millie Kingman's return. Besides lending a woman's hand in cleaning up the frightful wreckage the years had made, she'd even brought out from town a wagonload of worn but serviceable furniture to make the empty rooms less bleak and more nearly livable; and now Millie had added her own efforts, which included new curtains for all the windows. The result still looked enough like a poverty ranch, but at least one could tell that people lived here, and had pride in their surroundings.

Chantry carried Jess Kingman into one of the bedrooms, where a couple of roughly fashioned wooden bunks had been built against the walls. There he laid his partner gently on clean straw ticking, and with shaking hands worked at the buttons of the blood-drenched shirt. The tramp of his boots on uncarpeted boards had brought Millie hurrying from the kitchen. When he heard her sudden outcry in the door behind him, he tried hastily to shield Jess from his daughter's horrified gaze. But a glance at her face told him she had already seen; her eyes were tragic as she whispered, "Is — is he — ?"

"He's alive," Chantry answered. "That's all I do know." He felt the knotted pain in jaw muscles held too long clenched, and realized the tension he was under. He said harshly, "Can you find some towels or something, to try and stop this bleeding?"

Obediently she turned to fetch them. Chantry had the shirt ripped open now, and felt his mouth go dry at sight of the wound. The bullet had plowed through, low on the left side, and Kingman had been bleeding hard — though the flow seemed to have eased. As he was examining the wound, he heard a groan and saw that the hurt man's eyes were open. The lips, in a face gone pallid with bullet shock, stirred and spoke his name, faintly.

"Right here, Jess." He bent low, speaking loudly to make sure his words registered. "Jess, what happened? Who did it?"

"Garrett . . ." The tongue moved over dry lips.

Just then Millie was back with the towel Chantry had asked for. "Bring some water," he ordered. As she went for it he folded the towel over both mouths of the wound, lifting Kingman slightly to do so, and fetching another groan from him. Millie returned carrying a tin cup. Chantry slipped an arm behind the hurt man's shoulders as he put it to his lips. Kingman managed a couple of painful swallows, and then dropped back again.

He was still trying to speak. Making out the faint and broken words, Dal Chantry managed to piece together a story of missing Blaine cattle, of an encounter with Garrett and his men — of the foremen pulling a weapon on a man he knew to be unarmed, and Kingman's struggle to keep him from using it. The words ran out then and he realized Jess Kingman had lapsed into unconsciousness.

His face was bleak as he straightened and turned to the girl. He didn't try to dissemble. "I don't know much about such things as this. Do you?"

"No." Her lips formed the word but no sound came out.

He pulled off his hat, ran fingers through his hair. "It looks like a bad one to me. The bullet went through, but we haven't anything in the house to work with — not even so much as a bottle of whisky."

Millie said, "I've put water on to heat . . ."

"He needs something more than that. He needs a doctor."

"There isn't any in Oxbow."

Chantry came to a swift conclusion. "I'm gonna fetch Ada Starbuck. I have an idea shell know what's needed. Are you game to stay alone with him?"

"Of course," she assured him quickly. "And I'd feel much better if she were here. Only — please hurry!"

"I'll be as fast as I can," he promised, and turned out of the room with a purposeful stride.

In the barren living room he hesitated, looking at the table with its clutter of scraps and materials for Millie's project of curtain making. On a sudden decision he opened a drawer and took out the sixgun Ada Starbuck

72

had lent him. He checked the loads, shoved the gun behind his waistband and left the house.

Afterward he could only chafe at the time he was wasting as he stripped the gear from Jess Kingman's tired animal and turned it into the corral. Hurriedly he loaded his saddle onto his own, far fresher mount and swung onto its back, already setting the spurs. Millie was in the doorway to watch him leave; he lifted a hand in parting, as he swept out of the yard.

It was a thoroughly fagged horse that he rode into Oxbow, after what had seemed an interminable passage of time. He'd tried not to ask too much of the black but now, as he neared his destination, he became aware of the animal's heaving flanks and the sweat that ran from it. He drew in to let it sink its muzzle into a water trough; afterward, still impatient, he hurried on to the Starbuck store, and fumbled with the reins as he tied at the post outside. He felt as tired as the horse, his shoulders carrying a knotted weariness that he couldn't readily shake out of them. He pulled off his hat and was batting the dust from his clothing as he tramped inside the building.

Ada Starbuck was chatting with a townswoman while she wrapped a purchase. When she saw the look on Chantry's face she quickly brought the gossip to a halt, deftly snapping and tying the string and getting the customer outside and away. She closed the door as she exclaimed, "What is it? What's happened?"

"Jess's been hurt," he said, and saw her face lose color as he explained as briefly as possible. Even before he finished she was already turning briskly to the curtained doorway at the back of the store.

"I'll put some things together. Will you fetch the roan out of the shed?"

"You want the wagon?"

She shook her head. "Too slow. If you look around out there you'll see a saddle. I haven't used it in a coon's age, but I guess I haven't forgotten how."

"Yes, ma'am."

It was a clumsy looking sidesaddle, gathering dust on a rack. Dal Chantry found blanket and bridle and hurriedly piled the gear onto the roan, which submitted, though it was apparently some time since it had been ridden. When he led the horse around to the front of the store, Ada Starbuck was locking up. She wore her poke bonnet and shawl, and carried a pair of saddlebags into which, he saw, she had packed whatever she thought she would be needing. Chantry slung the bags into place behind the saddle, and then held a hand for her to step up to the roan's back.

As she settled herself, arranging her skirt, Chantry handed her the reins and said, "Can you make it alone? I used my bronc pretty hard coming in; I'm afraid we'd only hold you up. Besides," he added, as she bent a shrewdly probing look on him, "I'm not going straight back."

He saw her glance toward the gap of his coat, which had fallen open as he handed her into the saddle. Her eyes touched on the gun thrust behind his waistband, lifted again to his face; their expression was bleak. "What are you going to do?"

74

"A little chore," he answered curtly, and would say no more.

The woman's mouth tightened on further argument. She lifted the reins, speaking to the roan. She rode off, leaving Chantry standing beside his worn horse.

His throat was dry, and suddenly he knew he had to have a drink — his first since coming to the Oxbow — if he hoped to loosen the furious tensions inside him and the cramped ache in his shoulders. He rode to the nearest saloon, finding it empty at this slack hour of afternoon. The bartender on duty knew who he was, well enough, and gave him a cold and hostile stare; only when Chantry brought out his money and slapped it on the wood did the man reach for bottle and glass.

He had his drink, waiting to feel the heat of it strike through him. Tempted to a second shot, he looked at the bottle and at the empty glass in his hand but then he firmly shook his head. He set down the glass, aware of the watching eyes of the bartender as the latter swabbed away at a spotless area on the gleaming mahogany. Chantry settled his coat above the jutting gun handle and walked outside again to his horse.

Gone now was the frantic hurry that brought him pelting into town a half hour ago. It was replaced by a deliberate purpose. His head was clear, his turbulent emotions for the time, at least, in check.

The route he chose followed the main Valley road, the same one he had traveled in from Cross K. But there was a place some eight miles out of town where the ways forked; here he bore to the right, keeping to the more used wagon ruts instead of taking the neglected branch that led to the Kingman place. Now he was on unfamiliar ground, for it was the first time he'd been this way. The mood he was in, he felt he was riding deeper into enemy territory with every mile he covered.

He came to barbed wire, riding under a high gate from which a slab was hung bearing Luke Blaine's Broken Arrow brand burnt into it with a running iron. For another quarter hour he continued without seeing any further evidence he was on private land; then, abruptly, the wagon ruts twisted and dropped and a pleasant flat lay ahead. It was watered by a good-sized tributary of the Oxbow, and bottomed by stretches of meadow where he saw horses grazing against a rise of sheltering timber — pine mingled with aspen which must make a backdrop of pure gold in the autumn season.

Here stood Broken Arrow headquarters, solid looking buildings and a capacious layout of corrals; anyone could have seen it was an important ranch. It was dominated by the big house, part stone and part timber, with chimneys flanking either end of a steep-pitched roof. The veranda, deeply shaded with vines, looked out onto the whole reaching spread of the creek bottom.

The road crossed the creek on a plank bridge and then swung to merge with the bare, hoof-packed work area before the big barn. Dal Chantry pulled rein and looked around him. A warm wind swept the yard, carrying a tang of woodsmoke from the kitchen chimney, riffling the vines that hung thick around the porch of the house.

A voice said, "All right, Chantry! Turn that bronc and ride back the way you came — or else keep your hands in sight while you step out of the saddle!"

He turned his head. Ed Varner, the gunman, stood leaning against a pine trunk, a long-barreled Colt in one hand. Remembering what had happened that other time the two of them had met, Chantry could understand the leashed danger that burned in the man's stare — he wasn't apt to overlook the blow of a gunbarrel that had laid him low and sent him home jackknifed across the back of his horse. Chantry felt a tightening in his chest but he kept his voice firm and heavy with disdain. "Keep out of this, Varner," he said bluntly. "It has nothing to do with you."

The narrow face twisted with quick fury, but his answer was forestalled, for, over on the steps of the main house, Luke Blaine stood where he had emerged from the dark shadow of the vines. His voice carried as he demanded, "What's going on?" and then, recognizing Chantry: "Oh. It's you, is it?"

"Yeah. It's me," Chantry answered, and deliberately putting his back to Varner he walked his horse over to the foot of the steps. Drawing rein there, he looked past Blaine and now made out, dimly, the figure of a second man seated at a table on the porch; the brilliant sunlight shining directly in his face made it impossible to see who that man might be, but he kept a wary eye on him.

Luke Blaine, arms akimbo, looked at Chantry coldly. "If you've got business, state it. I'm a busy man."

"Too busy to talk to me about your crew coming over this afternoon and putting a bullet into Jess Kingman?"

The rancher stiffened, his head lifting as though with a shock of surprise. He repeated sharply, "Kingman? Is he dead?"

"Not dead. Though it's a wonder . . ."

The other seemed to reach a decision; with a summoning motion of his head he said, "Come up here," and turned back onto the porch.

Dal Chantry swung down. As his feet touched earth he felt the sudden thrust of a hard pressure against his back. He hadn't heard Ed Varner come up behind him but now the muzzle of Varner's sixshooter ground into his ribs and the gunman's voice said, "Not so fast!" As Chantry froze, a hand came around and jerked aside the front of his coat. The Colt was snatched from behind his waistband. "Now go up!" the voice said.

There was no use protesting. Chantry turned and gave the man a murderous look; a gun in each hand, Varner watched as he swung away and climbed the broad steps to the porch.

The vine covering made a pleasant green shade, and it looked as though he had interrupted a tranquil scene. Now Dal Chantry had a better look at the man who sat across the table from the chair that Blaine had vacated. He recognized the spare frame, the gold-rimmed spectacles and trimmed moustache of Clyde Humbird.

Seeing him more clearly than he had that night by lamplight in front of the Cross K house, he judged the man to be about thirty-five, with sandy hair receding from above a good, deep brow. He wore an Easterner's idea of riding clothes — tweed jacket and whipcord breeches, a shirt open at the throat. Fingers that looked as though they had never known physical labor toyed with a tall, moisture-beaded glass while the eyes behind the lenses regarded Chantry without emotion.

Luke Blaine made no move to offer the newcomer a chair, or a drink. He confronted Chantry. "Well?" he prodded truculently.

But a sound had drawn the latter's attention to the far end of the veranda, and to Gwen Macaulay seated there in the porch swing. She had on a frilly summer dress and held a book in her lap, closed on a finger to mark the place. She looked cool and, to Dal Chantry's staring eyes, completely beautiful. And why not, he reminded himself bitterly. Like her friend Humbird, she was someone on whom money had been lavished with nothing demanded in return. The book in her lap was probably the kind of three-decker novel that empty-headed women with nothing better to do liked to sit reading in porch swings on summer afternoons.

Somehow he didn't believe any of this. Even if she did belong in the effete Eastern background that produced a man like Clyde Humbird, there was still something solid and worthwhile about her, something he could sense, merely from the level and concerned regard she gave him now.

Her uncle was losing his temper. "You've got something to tell me?" he demanded, and brought Chantry's eyes belatedly back to him.

He let him have it briefly: "Garrett, and I don't know how many more of your crew, ran across Jess Kingman today, alone on his own range. There were some words — something about some cattle they accused him of taking. Garrett pulled a gun and shot Jess, damned near gut shot him. His horse brought him home."

Luke Blaine's stare was like a thunderclap. His chest stirred to a drawn breath and he said heavily, "You sure you're giving me the whole story? And a true one?"

"There might be more to it," Chantry conceded brittly. "That's as much as Jess was able to tell me. If you think I'm lying —"

"I did send Ford over there today," Blaine interrupted. "With orders to collect Broken Arrow stock and move it back onto Broken Arrow grass."

This was so unexpected that Dal Chantry was taken aback. He actually blinked, and Luke Blaine read his surprise correctly. "You seem to find that hard to believe," he snapped. "It happens to be the truth! It was a peaceful mission. And maybe you expect *me* to believe that, without any kind of provocation —"

He broke off, his head swinging about as a knot of riders came spurring into the ranch yard. It was Clyde Humbird who said, "Here's Garrett now. You can ask him."

"I mean to," Blaine said gruffly, and from the top of the steps yelled his foreman's name.

Ford Garrett heard and, leaving his men to dismount in a scatter of raised dust near the barn, spurred over and dropped from the saddle. He came tramping up the steps, halting with a look of sudden danger as he caught sight of the visitor. His glance flicked across Chantry, and then sought his employer. "Yeah?"

"What happened between you and Kingman?"

Understanding darkened the foreman's stare. He looked challengingly at Chantry as he answered. "We had some words. He called me something I don't ordinarily take off any man — but I was trying to follow orders. Then he went for a gun and I shot him. His horse carried him off."

"Jess doesn't own a gun," Chantry retorted. "The only one we have between us is that sixgun Ed Varner just took from me — and that was lying in a table drawer, in the Cross K living room. So how could he have drawn on you?"

Garrett met the challenge, a muscle leaping in the corner of his truculent, outthrust jaw. Luke Blaine was watching him, waiting for his answer. Instead, Garrett turned and shouted to the quartet of cowhands who had dismounted yonder at the barn. "Slim! Hackett! All four of you come over here."

They crossed the yard, leather chaps flapping about their legs. They halted at the foot of the steps, and Ford Garrett stabbed a pointing finger at them as he said loudly, "You were with me when I had that trouble with Kingman today. I want you to tell the boss: did he or did he not have a gun, and did he try to use it first? How about it?"

Silence hung on the answer. The men took their time, passing a look among them as though each waited for the next to speak up. Then one said gruffly, "That's right. He pulled first." And the others solemnly nodded.

Garrett's chest swelled and a grin of triumph broke across his face. He spread his hands as he looked at Blaine who, in turn, put his cold stare on Dal Chantry.

"Anything more you want to say?"

Chantry was having trouble with his breathing, aware of the old, familiar sensation of iron bands tightening about his chest, the blood pumping hotly against the very roof of his skull. His hands knotted, up; but with the controls that he was slowly learning to bring upon his temper he managed somehow to do so now. His voice when he spoke didn't sound like his own.

"I reckon not," he told Blaine harshly. "I reckon there ain't a damn bit of use in it. It was a waste of time, my even riding over here! But if Jess dies from that bullet," he added, and his hot stare swept to. Garrett's grinning face, settled there. "If he dies — I promise you'll be seeing me again!"

He swung away and strode down the steps, the men at the bottom quickly splitting and fading aside to let him pass through. He went directly to his horse and in a dead silence caught up the reins, found the stirrup.

Once in the saddle he looked about, seeking and now locating Ed Varner standing a little apart. He sent the black walking directly toward him; Varner stood his ground until the last moment. Then something seemed to flicker in his eyes and he broke and fell back a step

— and it seemed to Dal Chantry that this one movement betrayed a weakness of nerve in the gunman that he might never have suspected. It gave him his one moment of triumph in this whole miserable encounter.

He urged the black closer until, protesting, the animal tossed its head and fought the bit. He reined in, then, with the nose of the horse almost touching Ed Varner's chest. Leaning slightly forward he told the gunman, "You got something belongs to me. Hand it over."

For a moment the black eyes held his own, but Varner had already broken once and now his stare slid away. With a savage motion he dragged the sixgun out from behind his belt and handed it up, butt first. Chantry took it. Afterward, yanking the black away, he gave it the spur and rode from there — head up and shoulders straight, trying to show these people a pride and an arrogance that they would remember.

He didn't once look back.

CHAPTER
EIGHT

A word to Garrett and the other hands dismissed them, and Luke Blaine turned back to face his niece and Clyde Humbird, neither of whom had moved. The Broken Arrow owner's fists were clenched, his face dark with angry color. "That jailbird!" he gritted. "By God, some day he's going to find he can push me too far!"

Humbird picked up his drink and finished it. Looking into the empty glass he said mildly, "Those chaps of yours were lying, you know."

Slowly Blaine's head lifted and turned. "What was that?"

"They were lying," the Easterner repeated, "when they said this fellow Kingman made the first move toward a gun. It was perfectly obvious Garrett had coached them in what to say — but he apparently didn't do a very good job of it."

Incredulity and astonishment gave place to fresh anger in Blaine's dark face. "Would you expect me to believe crooks like Chantry and Kingman? Against my own men?"

Humbird considered and shook his head. "No," he said. "I suppose not. Just the same, I can't help but think Chantry told the truth."

84

The rancher seemed to swell with quick fury; his mouth went white at the corners. When he spoke it was with an obvious effort at self-control. "Let me tell you something! You're a pretty smart young fellow. But with all due respect, you're still only a guest on this ranch. It ain't your country — you don't know what a man has to do to look after his interests, here where the law is no more than what he makes it. I suggest you just sort of keep your advice to yourself, and let me run Broken Arrow's affairs as I figure I know best how to do. Is that all right?"

Clyde Humbird looked up at the angry face above him. After a moment he nodded. "Why, of course," he said, his voice calm. "Perfectly all right with me . . ."

Another awkward moment, and then Luke Blaine went stomping into the house. Of the two who remained there on the porch, neither spoke at first. Then Gwen said seriously, "I'm awfully sorry. He didn't mean to insult you, Clyde. It's simply his way."

"I know." The Easterner added, in an odd tone, "Don't worry about it. I think I'm just finally beginning to understand his way. I suppose, perhaps, it's a good thing."

The girl frowned, sitting up a little straighter. "I wish I knew what you meant by that . . ."

Not answering, he set aside his empty glass with a sigh and rose abruptly, as though forming a sudden resolution. "Will you excuse me? I think there's a ride I have to take."

Remembering that the black had been hard-pushed for the whole distance to town and then to Broken Arrow, Dal Chantry fought his impatience and set an easier pace on his ride home. He found Ada Starbuck's horse, still under saddle, waiting at the front door; and, hurrying inside, he met Millie Kingman just coming from her father's room and putting a finger to her lips as Chantry burst into the house. "How is he?" Chantry demanded.

"Resting," she said. "Perhaps he'll sleep; Ada's going to sit with him awhile to make certain he doesn't want for anything. She's really a wonder!" the girl went on. "A doctor couldn't have done better. She thinks he's going to be fine, if he just stays quiet and lets things mend."

It was the first good news Chantry had heard, and suddenly relief poured through him, easing the tensions and frustrations, almost taking the starch out of him so that he had to stiffen his knees to prevent their trembling. He nodded briefly, said gruffly, "That's fine. Really fine!"

The girl looked at him with a troubled frown. "Are you all right?" she faltered. And at his nod she added hesitantly, "We — wondered where you might have gone to, all this time . . ."

"I'll tell you about it later," he said, already turning away. "Right now I better see to those horses."

He escaped with that and went out and led his own black and Ada's roan around to the corral, where he stripped the gear and turned them in to feed and water.

The black could use a rubdown but he decided to let that go for now. He stood in the barn door, watching the sun lean toward the western ridges while shadows stretched long through the last wine-glow of afternoon. A hundred troubled thoughts chased through his mind; it hardly seemed it could have been just hours ago that he had been up on the roof, doing a peaceful job of repair and enjoying the sight of brand-new shingles gleaming under his hammer. It was almost like another life, another place. Now the road ahead looked dangerous and uncertain.

Suddenly he stiffened. No doubt of it, this was a day for visitors at Cross K ranch house. He walked out into the yard, watching the horseman he could see approaching along the bottom road. There was still sufficient light to show him clearly and when he was near enough to be recognized as the Easterner, Clyde Humbird, Chantry could only scowl in disbelief.

He walked forward then, going out to meet Humbird as the latter came to a halt near the house. Chantry stared at the man, trying to fathom some reason for his being here at all. He said gruffly, "You got here almost before I did!"

The bluntness of his words must have caused the stain of color that spread quickly through the man's smooth cheek. Humbird frowned and touched the knuckle of a forefinger to his clipped moustache. He said, "I suppose it must look as though I'm meddling in things that don't concern me, at that. If so, then I'm sorry. But after what you told us this afternoon at Broken Arrow, I couldn't help but feel concerned. I liked what little I saw of this Jess Kingman. I wanted to know how he's doing."

He sounded sincere, and Chantry shrugged and answered, "Far as I can tell he's doing well enough. It's a bad wound, but not fatal."

"I'm glad to hear it," Humbird said. He added, "May I speak to him?"

Chantry's eyes narrowed a little, his cheeks pinching up. "I can't think of any good reason you should."

"All the same," the man said patiently, "I'd like to talk to him. To both of you."

The other, after hesitating, found he could offer no good objection. "I'll leave it up to Miz Starbuck," he said finally. "If she thinks it's all right . . . Come inside."

"Thanks," the Easterner said, dismounting. Seeing him for the first time on his feet, Chantry discovered he was a bigger man than he had suspected, and wider through the shoulders. Despite the gold-rimmed glasses and the neat moustache and the general grooming, he suspected there might be more to this man than he had been inclined to think.

Looking around him before he stepped up to the porch, Clyde Humbird said in a tone of approval, "You must have been working hard. I see a lot of change here, and in only a few days."

"It's been a job, all right," Chantry said, brushing aside the compliment. He stood back and let Humbird precede him into the house.

Millie sat at the living room table, working at her curtains — more likely than not merely trying to occupy herself and take her mind off her father's plight. Ada Starbuck stood at a window, her capable arms folded, looking off toward a timbered ridge that swam in late afternoon light. They both showed their puzzlement. Chantry made brief introductions, Clyde Humbird nodding politely with hat in hand.

Ada looked at him speculatively, her graying head tipped to one side. "Yeah, I've heard of you," she said with her native directness. "House guest at Broken Arrow — someone the Macaulay girl knew back East. I been wondering just what you looked like." She added, "I hear you two are getting married."

Chantry hoped his face didn't show anything as he heard this. Humbird, for his part, merely let a corner of his mouth tilt beneath the trim moustache. "Why, I suppose you can always hear a good many things about strangers," he commented pleasantly. "Some of them premature, at the least."

Dal Chantry cut in gruffly, "Humbird thinks he wants a word with Jess, for some reason which he ain't explained. I said I'd ask you."

"Well —" Ada frowned, plainly as puzzled by the request as Chantry was. Hesitating, she said, "If you're sure it's important — I'll see if he's awake and feels up to it."

"Please," the Easterner said. "I consider it important." She disappeared into the bedroom. There followed an awkward moment of waiting, during which Millie Kingman looked at the stranger in perplexity and a low murmur of voices reached them through the thin partition. The door opened again and Ada was there nodding. Clyde Humbird thanked her and moved past her through the door, Dal Chantry directly behind him.

Jess Kingman lay on his bunk, hands folded on top of the blanket and a look of patient resignation on his face. It seemed to Chantry that pain had dulled his eyes and sunk his cheeks; the flesh of his face looked gray and dry as paper.

The eyes rested on Humbird. The colorless lips stirred and the effort of speech seemed to take reserves of hoarded strength. "I reckon — you'll excuse me if I don't get up," he said faintly, and added, "Ada tells me you asked to see me about something."

"That's true," the Easterner said, looking around. Dal Chantry guessed he was seeking a chair. There was only one, against the wall, and Chantry hooked it with a toe and pulled it out for him. Humbird thanked him and placed the chair by the bed, where he seated himself and laid his hat on his knee. "It seems you've had a close call . . ."

"Close enough," Kingman admitted.

Dal Chantry, still standing near the foot of the wooden bunkframe, cut in on him. "Jess ain't exactly in the best shape to listen to small talk, mister. If you've got some reason for being here, taking up his time, maybe you'll be good enough to get to the point!"

"Very well," Humbird said, matching the crispness of Chantry's manner. "Though I may not be able to make it very brief . . . First, I don't know just what you've heard about me, but it's probably fairly close to the facts: I'm a friend of Gwen Macaulay's, that she knew in Philadelphia. I'm unattached, irresponsible, and I

90

have more money than is probably good for me. But the money came from my father, and I would prefer to earn some of my own — that is, if I knew the trick of doing it.

"Gwen and I have been in correspondence since she came West, and what she told me about this Montana country had me so intrigued that I finally invited myself to visit at Broken Arrow. I've liked everything I've seen. In fact, you may laugh at this, but I have a strong feeling that there's a place for me in this cattle business."

He paused for a reaction. Jess Kingman waited in silence, but Chantry, his dislike unconcealed, commented dryly, "I guess to somebody like you that's all it *would* look like — a business. But to people here, it's something more than that. It's a way of life."

Humbird merely looked at him. "I'm quite sure of that," he said quietly, and turned again to the man in the bunk. Chantry didn't know why he felt as though he had been reprimanded.

The Easterner continued: "I've been having some discussions with Mr. Blaine about the possibility of putting some of my money into Broken Arrow — I gather that even a successful rancher can have so much of his capital tied up in livestock and equipment that it may mean going to the bank when he wants to plan improvements to his herd or his land. A deal has been suggested whereby I'd be cut in for a small share of Broken Arrow, in return for the investment. But —" He hesitated, as though searching for words. "Something has happened, today, that makes it seem unlikely I can work with Blaine. I think I'm going to have to look elsewhere."

Jess Kingman was frowning at the man, as though he were ranging ahead of the words and puzzled by what he found there. He said now, "Are you going to tell us you came here with some kind of a business proposition? Knowing who and what we are?"

Humbird admitted it with a nod. "I also know what I see. I like spirit. I like the kind of man who will walk up to an enemy and have it out with him — as I saw at Broken Arrow today . . ." He looked at Chantry briefly. "This is what I propose," he went on. "According to Luke Blaine, you've got the makings of a good ranch. But your range is empty, with no way in the world for you to stock it. Well, perhaps I have the money to buy the beef you need."

"You're serious?" Jess Kingman exclaimed, and looked at Chantry.

The latter was scowling, blunt jaw set firm, the muscles knotted in his cheeks.

He said sharply, "And what do you want out of this? A full partnership, I reckon — maybe even a mortgage against the ranch, so you can figure to end up taking over the whole spread. Jess, be carefull For all you know Blaine could have sent him!"

Humbird considered him without animosity. "I'd think rather less of you if you weren't suspicious. But, no. This is an honest offer I'm making, with no strings attached — and nothing to do with Luke Blaine. I mean to put no claim against the ranch. I'll stock your range, on shares, and pay for a crew if you need one. I'll give you a fair split of the profit on the market price, and terms on whatever part you decide to keep in order to build up a herd. We'll have the whole thing put down in black and white, if that will please you better."

"And what do you get from the deal?" Kingman asked.

"Experience. I expect to be given a chance to learn about the actual operation of the ranch. I won't try to take over where I'm not equipped to; but I do count on being consulted and treated with due consideration as a business associate. That, I know now, is something I could never hope for from Luke Blaine. He has consideration for no one but himself!

"One other thing: I'd have to insist that every effort be made to avoid trouble with Blaine or any other neighbor. After all, I hardly feel I can afford to invest in a range war! In particular, I'd want you to call off this business of impounding other men's cattle, and instead see that they are rounded up and returned to their own range . . ."

Abruptly, the man slapped a hand against his knee and stood. "Well, I've talked enough. There's my offer — you'll want to think about it and discuss it between yourselves. Just let me know what you decide." He added, "I hope you'll be on your feet again, in good time."

"Thanks," Kingman said. He glanced at Dal Chantry. "If you could leave us two alone for a few minutes, we might have an answer for you right quick."

Clyde Humbird nodded, and walked from the room. Chantry stepped and closed the door. When he turned back, his mouth was set firm and his eyes were smoldering; looking at him Kingman said, "You're against taking his offer?"

Chantry exploded. "Who does he think he is, laying down terms to us? And why does he want to do business with a pair of jailbirds anyway? What's really up his sleeve? I don't trust him!"

Suddenly Jess Kingman looked very tired. He put up a hand and ran the palm across his cheeks where it rasped over gray beard stubble. He gazed straight overhead at the cracked plaster of the ceiling. "I dunno, boy. Like I said once, you don't trust anyone. Could be you're right not to. But somehow, I like this man — and just now what other choice have we got?"

And he drew a breath and closed his eyes a moment, as though bracing to meet the onslaught of arguments he knew he was about to endure.

Despite the grainy dusk flooring the Valley of the Oxbow, Gwen Macaulay was sure she recognized that saddled horse standing before the Cross K ranch house; coming nearer, she saw it clearly in lamplight from a window, and found she was right. Because of the time it had taken her to change to riding costume — and to make up her mind that it was proper to follow him — she could only guess what direction Clyde Humbird had ridden after that dreadful scene on the veranda; but her instinct had led her here, and her instinct had been correct.

Now, as she rode up and dismounted, dropping her pony's reins, the door of the house opened and Clyde

94

himself stepped out. He was hatless in the chill spring evening, and she thought he looked perturbed. He halted in surprise as Gwen came up onto the porch beside him. "Gwen?" he said into the thickening dusk.

She said quickly, by way of explanation, "I guess we both had the same impulse, after hearing what happened to that poor Mr. Kingman. You've seen him, Clyde? Is he badly hurt?"

"He seems to be doing fairly well," he said. "Considering. Mrs. Starbuck's inside. You know her, I suppose. But you haven't met the daughter . . ."

"The one they were hunting for that night? I'd like very much to meet her."

But he put a hand on her arm, halting her as she would have turned to the door. "First," he said, "there's something I want to explain if I can. It may not be easy."

A troubled note in his voice made her look closely at him. "What is it, Clyde?"

He ran a palm across crisp blond hair. "You may not like the real reason I came here tonight. I know your uncle won't."

"In the first place," she interrupted, "you don't owe my uncle anything. You've been *my* guest, not his. And after the way I heard him talk to you —"

"That didn't matter. The thing is, I feel a little responsible for what happened today. After all, I was the one who insisted he should be told Jess Kingman was back — and the very next day he sent his men here to Cross K and there was trouble. Since then, one thing has led to another . . . But I suppose that's all beside the point. The thing is, I've just been talking to Kingman and to that young Chantry fellow. And I've made them an offer."

She was staring at him in the faint flow of light from the window as he hastily explained the details of the proposition he had laid before the Cross K partners. He finished: "I'm sure that your Uncle Luke would say I was a traitor — offering to help these men. And if the thing goes through, he'll have you to thank for bringing me into the picture."

"I'm not afraid of Uncle Luke," she said quickly. "And I'm certainly not angry with you. But — just exactly why did you want to do this? Really, I'm curious."

"Well, after all, I think I'm a business man. This looks like a good proposition to me."

"I wonder . . ." She shook her head a little, looking at this man she had thought she knew well enough. "*Is* it business? Or are you someone who just has to give a hand to the underdog?"

She couldn't be sure, but she thought a stain of color darkened his cheeks. He shrugged as he said, "Well, maybe nothing will come of it. I'm not at all sure they mean to take me up on my offer. Young Chantry, I'm certain, thinks I'm trying to cheat them — they were arguing so loudly that I got embarrassed and came out here to get away from the sound of it." The lenses of his eyeglasses glinted as he shook his head; his tone was faintly bitter. "I always *try* to do the right thing, but more than likely I've only made a mess of it again . . ."

Gwen suddenly placed a hand on his arm. "Hold still, Clyde," she said. "I'm going to kiss you!"

"What! You don't mean to say you've finally —"

"No, Clyde," she said, though she knew she was disappointing him. "I'm sorry. Not that — but just because you're one of the really nicest people I know."

Resignation in his voice, he answered, "At least it's nice you think *that* much of me." And then, on her impulse of sympathy and liking, she lifted her mouth and his hands touched her waist in a respectful embrace as their lips met and held. They were like that when the door opened. Stepping back quickly, Gwen turned and saw the man called Dal Chantry staring, a black look on him.

For a moment no one spoke as an odd sort of constraint seemed to bother all three. It was Gwen who finally spoke. "Good evening. I came to see about Mr. Kingman. I — hope you don't mind."

The young man's words were gruff, as though roughened with emotion. "It's all right," he said. "It's right kind of you. Come in." He turned his head, his stare cutting to the other man. "You too, Humbird," he added grudgingly, in a tone that held no real friendliness. "We done our talking. You win. We're ready to discuss terms."

He stepped back, holding the door for them. His face, in the lamplight that flooded out, was dark with feeling.

CHAPTER
NINE

For all the promise of financial help from Clyde Humbird, the fact remained that at the moment Dal Chantry faced a mountain of labor and he faced it alone. Aside from the job of pushing off the cattle of other brands that didn't belong there, an uncounted number of things had to be done to prepare Cross K range for the stock that Humbird had promised. And there were the neglected irrigation ditches Jess Kingman had, long ago, put in to lead Oxbow water onto his hay fields — if there was any hope of getting a cutting of winter feed this season, these must be cleaned put and put in order.

Boneweary and discouraged — a normal state of affairs with him these days — he rode in to the noon meal and saw Millie Kingman signaling to him from the door of the house. Stabbed by a quick alarm at the thought that it must mean Jess had taken a bad turn, he spurred over there; but to his stammered question the girl hurriedly shook her head. "Oh, no, Dal. Nothing like that. Papa's resting well."

"Then what's wrong?" he demanded gruffly, and saw her gentle smile.

"Why does it always have to be something wrong? You're such a pessimist, Dal!" She quickly went on to explain: "A couple of men rode in a few minutes ago. They said they saw Mr. Humbird in town and he hired them on, to ride for you."

Chantry straightened in the saddle. "It's about time!" he grunted. Something in her expression made him add, "What do you think of them?"

"Well, I — just don't know." Her hesitation only helped confirm his own sour judgment of the kind of man the inexperienced Clyde Humbird would hire. Scowling, he looked around.

"Where are they?"

She nodded toward the barn. "I told them to take care of their horses."

Chantry pulled the black about and headed him in that direction.

There were, he saw now, a couple of strange broncs in the barn corral working at the hay in the rick. Riding nearer Chantry sized them up, and also the saddles racked on the top pole; they told him little enough — nondescript mounts, nondescript rigs. Still no sign of the owners. He dismounted, throwing the reins for an anchor, and walked into the barn.

A voice at his back said, "Hi, kid."

He stiffened and slowly turned. Coming into the quiet gloom of the big barn's interior, he'd walked right past without seeing them. They were in shadow at either side of the big door, one lounging at his ease on the lid of a tack box, the other standing against the rough wall with a burning cigarette hanging from his mouth. He spoke again as Dal Chantry merely stared without answering; the cigarette bobbed to the movement of his lips. "Hey, now! You ain't forgetting old friends?"

Scowling, Dal Chantry drew a breath. "Where did you two come from?"

Ollie Brice straightened, pulling away from the wall; he took the cigarette from his mouth and snapped it through the archway to the dust outside. He was medium-sized, stocky of build, with untrimmed wheat-straw hair and a straggling moustache that was oddly light against the saddle-dark skin of his face. A sixgun rode the holster at his thigh.

"We come across half of Montana. Was over toward Deer Lodge, and heard about you being turned loose. Heard that you and the other feller you got sprung with had started west, likely heading for the Oxbow. So we strung along after."

"Why?"

Chantry's rejoinder, wholly without warmth or welcome, caused redheaded Mort Jennings to lean forward on the bin where he sat, a frown on his crafty, foxlike face. "Why, for old times' sake, kid. We thought you'd be glad to know we hadn't forgotten you — after that tough break we all ran into four years ago over at Miles."

"Why would you want to remember somebody, after you ran out on him the way you did me?" Dal Chantry reminded him bitterly.

Mort Jennings looked positively shocked and grieved. "What are you saying, kid? You don't think we *liked* leaving you with that posse! But once they got their hands on you, wasn't a damn thing the two of us could have done."

"All right." He let it go with an angry shrug.

Ollie Brice was studying him from under his pale brows and shaking his head. "I can't see any reason you should hold a grudge after all this time," he said. "Look at Mort and me — still riding the grubline, still picking up a dime wherever we can, no better off than we ever was. But, you, now: you got things by the tail!"

Chantry gave him a stare. "Yeah?"

The blond man made a sweeping gesture that indicated the silence of the barn where they stood, the ranch buildings, the acres of bunch grass stretching away toward hills and river bottom. "Why, hell! Look at all this — half of it yours, according to what we was told."

"You been busy asking questions about me, sounds like!"

"Well, ain't it natural we'd be interested?"

Mort Jennings unfolded his lean length off the top of the bin. He always moved, Chantry remembered, with a deceptive indolence; actually there was a wary, cocked intensity about the man — you could read it in the eyes, in the look of the narrow, pointed face. He took papers and tobacco sack from a pocket of his black-and-red checkered shirt now as he said, "I don't see what call you got to talk tough with us, kid. You got nothing to bitch about. Looks to me you've made a pretty fair trade — for a few years that you ain't really gonna miss."

"That's how it looks to you, is it?" It might be easy to say, he thought bitterly, if you hadn't been the one who actually paid the price — the years of prison stench and prison labor, the hard confinement that cracked the spirit and corroded the fiber of a man. But he saw no point in pressing the matter, so he shrugged and said gruffly, "Let it go."

"Why, sure," Ollie Brice agreed, grinning. "We got nothing to fight about. The two of us are working for you now, kid. Run into that fellow in town — dude called Hummingbird, or whatever the hell his name is. He told us he was hiring a crew for you. When he heard about us being old friends, he was real glad to sign us on."

Chantry considered them both for a long moment before he nodded resignedly. "All right. I don't even know if you two ever done any actual work in your lives — but if it's what you're looking for I can promise you'll find it here! You'll punch cattle, you'll string wire, you'll clean ditches. And if you want a place to sleep, you'll begin right now by fixing up the bunkshack and making it so you can live in it. You'll work as many hours as I do, and you'll take my orders with no back talk. Do your job and maybe then I'll forget about what happened at Miles City. That all clear?"

The two drifters exchanged a look; it was Ollie Brice who said, grinning blandly, "Why sure, kid. You're the boss, ain't you? We never figured otherwise."

Chantry nodded, started to turn away. "When you've washed up, come in the house and we'll see what Millie has on the stove for dinner . . ."

"The girl, you mean?" The tone of the question made Chantry look back sharply. Brice's grin had broadened until his eyes were nearly lost in the folds of broad cheeks. "I said you had things by the tail. What is she, a bonus? A little scrawny for my taste — but a looker, all right!"

Fierce outrage made Chantry's voice tremble and his hands bunch into fists as he swung about to face the man. "Another thing: that was the last remark of that kind I want to hear, you understand? Millie Kingman has nothing at all to do with you. First one of you that goes near her gets a licking hell never forget!"

The grin vanished, leaving the blond man's eyes completely cold as they deliberately measured Chantry. "You think you could give me a licking?" he asked, too quietly.

But even as he said it there was an edge of uncertainty in the words, as though what he saw in the young fellow took some of the mocking sureness from him. His glance slid past, sought Mort Jennings briefly; when he got no help from the redhead's watchful stare he looked again at Chantry and the vacuous grin was back. "Aw, hell! Take it easy! Man should be able to tell when he's being ribbed. We wouldn't try to horn in on your personal territory."

"And it ain't like that, either!" Dal Chantry exploded, and felt the heat rush into his face. "You just remember what I said — that's all. And let it end there!"

"Sure," Mort Jennings put in seriously, nodding his red head. "Don't mind Ollie, kid. He didn't mean nothing. He was trying to be funny . . ."

Dal Chantry, still boiling, decided he would have to settle for that.

With three pairs of hands to do the work — even if two of them belonged to a crew he had been reluctant to accept — Chantry for the first time saw some encouraging hope of catching up. Once he'd laid down the law, Brice and Jennings proved tractable and carried out his orders willingly enough.

He began to let down the bars a little and actually to feel, for the first time, something of the pleasure he figured he should be experiencing in working on his own spread, building his own future. Jess Kingman continued to improve, under the care of his daughter and the faithful Ada Starbuck, who was neglecting her store in her wish to do everything possible for him. And one day Clyde Humbird rode out to find out how the new hands he had hired were making out, and to announce that he had been dickering by wire with a Wyoming dealer for six hundred head of feed stock to serve as the beginning of the herd. As soon as negotiations were completed and a price agreed on, the cattle would be driven up and put on Cross K grass.

This all sounded good; being honest with himself, Dal Chantry had to admit that his suspicion and dislike of the Easterner fed chiefly on one thing — the memory of a moment when he'd stumbled across Humbird and Gwen Macaulay on the porch of the Cross K house, and of a kiss that still made him tremble with jealousy.

He couldn't help it . . . it was just something he had to learn to live with.

In two days he and his men had gathered every head of Luke Blaine's Broken Arrow cattle that had been on Cross K range — except for the missing seventeen head which he hadn't had time to look for but which, once driven into the hills, Chantry figured were probably past recovery. On an afternoon when thunderheads piled high on the western ridges and the air was sultry and electric with a threatening storm, they pushed a final jog of Blaine cattle across the dry creek bed which marked, roughly, the boundary between the two spreads. There had been a fence here at one time but it had long since been pulled down. Chantry pointed to what remained of the posts, lying in a haphazard line and turning silver with age. He told his men, "We got a shipment of wire coming. When it gets here, this fence goes up again. And this time it stays up!"

Mort Jennings said, "Maybe there's somebody yonder who might think different. They seem pretty damned interested in us."

Chantry twisted in the saddle to follow the direction of his-nod. A pair of riders had drawn up on a knoll on Broken Arrow's side of the boundary. Dal Chantry recognized the big roan under the larger of the men before he knew the rider. It was Ford Garrett, all right, and sudden eagerness sang along his nerves, heightening his pulse. This was the first time since the shooting of his partner that he had had a chance to confront Jess Kingman's assailant on anything like equal terms.

Almost without thinking, and without a word to his companions, he lifted the reins and kicked the black forward.

It took the dry wash at a couple of bounds, and then Chantry was riding deliberately toward the Broken Arrow riders who held their places and watched him come. That was the gunman, Ed Varner, on the second horse, Chantry saw now. But his eye was filled with the man he hated, and the electric tension of the threatened storm only seemed to heighten his recklessness.

The last straggling steers scattered out of his way and then he was pulling rein to confront the Broken Arrow foreman. Chantry indicated the drifting cattle and said flatly, "There's your boss's beef, Garrett. All of it. After this, keep it where it belongs!"

The deepset eyes returned his stare; Garrett's full lips tilted in a sneer. "I don't run Broken Arrow to your specifications. And I don't take orders from no punk jailbird."

Despite the explosion of anger going off inside his head, Dal Chantry somehow managed to keep his voice steady, his movements deliberate. "Here's one you'll take!" he said curtly, and dropping the reins across his horse's neck he swung down to the ground. "We got a score to settle. Get off that horse!"

The big man only looked at him. "I'd bust you in two, kid!"

"I'll give you the chance. You apparently don't mind shooting unarmed old men out of their saddles. Well — try your luck on me!"

106

Garrett seemed tempted; but then he shook his head with a sneer. "Some other time, maybe."

"*Now!*"

"You go to the devil . . ."

The Broken Arrow foreman started to back and pivot the big gelding. Suddenly Chantry was lunging forward, all the pent-up fury exploding in blind, furious action. He hurled himself at Garrett, grabbing at the arm the latter raised to fend him off. His other hand caught a fistful of vest and shirtfront. He took a blow, backhanded, full across the face but wouldn't break his grip. Then the horse started to sidle nervously away, and the big man let out a yell as he felt the seat go from under him. Chantry set his heels in the sandy soil and gave a heave, and all at once Ford Garrett's heavy bulk was coming down on him.

He managed to back away a couple of chopping steps to keep from being carried under as Garrett was dumped on his back. At once the big man came bouncing and rolling up to his feet, bawling with rage, while his right paw slapped for the holster strapped about his middle. Chantry's gun — the one Ada Starbuck had given him — was in his saddle roll; he could only stand helpless as those other fingers curled about the revolver's grip. But they froze there, the gun drawn, for a voice above and behind Chantry said sharply, "Broken Arrow! Leave the guns where they are — both of you!"

Chantry looked around. He had been no more than dimly aware of pounding hooves shaking the ground; in his single-minded fury he had forgotten Ollie Brice and

Mort Jennings. What was more important, he had even forgotten the menace of Ed Varner, on that other Broken Arrow mount. But now, for the moment, the danger was averted.

Varner had heeded Brice's warning. He sat motionless, poised and dangerous, staring into the muzzle of the blond rider's gun; his black eyes held murder but he must have recognized this was a time for caution. And now, as the scene held, Mort Jennings kicked his ugly bronc and walked him around the other side of Varner's where he lifted the Colt from the gunman's holster and tossed it aside into the bunch grass. Continuing, he came to Garrett and, leaning from saddle, knocked the foreman's hand away from his gunbutt and plucked the weapon free. Straightening, he told Chantry, "All right, kid. There he is if you want him. Go ahead . . ."

But it was Ford Garrett who, with a roar, came charging to the battle like a mastiff let off the leash — all his arrogance gone now — in a blind need to get his hands on this man twenty years his junior who had dared to dump him from the saddle.

For all the differences in their ages, Garrett was tough and he was solid; and, for his bulk, he was swift. He took his opponent by surprise, sent him reeling under the unexpected weight of a solid blow to the chest. But Chantry caught himself, dug in and flung up an arm that blocked the fist aimed at his head. As the foreman slammed into him, his own right drove for the man's thick middle, seemed to sink in up to his wrist. Breath, rank with tobacco smell, gusted from the man's gaping mouth. He stopped in his tracks for the moment. And Dal Chantry, moving back a pace, flung his second blow directly at the unprotected face and felt flesh give beneath his knuckles.

They went at it then, toe-to-toe, two well-matched foes, enraged and giving no quarter. There was no cheering from the three onlookers, no sound at all except the slogging of fists and scrape of boots, the panting of laboring lungs, the slur of hooves as a horse moved out of the way. The fight raged all over the crest of that shallow knoll while, unheeded, a small chill wind began to blow from the line of stormclouds on the horizon, whipping away the gritty dust they kicked up.

When Dal Chantry caught a warning cry — from Ollie Brice, he thought — he was able to give it little attention. He didn't know if what he heard was other horsemen approaching or the pound of his own pulse in his ears. He was nearly blinded by the freely flowing blood from a cut opened over one eye. The shirt was half torn from his back, his whole side was stabbed with pain at every breath — when he was down a lashing kick from one of Ford Garrett's heavy cowhide boots had caught him before he could roll away, and in his dazed condition he wasn't sure but what a rib might have been cracked.

But Garrett was taking even worse punishment. Both eyes were swollen and his nose had been flattened, and he whined like an animal with every painfully gasping breath. He crouched like an animal, too, the massive shoulders sloping and the thick knees bent as he sought to bring his elusive enemy within the grip of those crushing arms. Perhaps the years were beginning to tell on him. He came on, though, no more willing than Chantry to call for quarter. And every blow that landed was, for the younger man, payment for the lies that had sent Jess Kingman to prison, and the bullet that had sent Jess Kingman home to Cross K, clinging to the saddle, near to death . . .

Suddenly Chantry's fist struck empty air and the impetus of his own reach almost dropped him on his face. He caught himself and stood swaying and breathing with effort while he looked about for his enemy. He found him, lying on his face in the dirt, arms and legs sprawling. Staring blearily down at him, Dal Chantry felt thwarted and cheated. "Get up!" he shouted hoarsely. "Damn it, you can't quit on me!"

From somewhere a long way off Mort Jennings said, "Kid, he's out cold. He's finished."

"The devil he is!" He dropped to his knees, grabbed Garrett by his clothing and with almost the last of his strength rolled the man over on his back. Garrett's eyes were closed, his mouth agape. His head lolled as Chantry shook him furiously. "Get up!" the young fellow repeated witlessly. "Damn it, *I* ain't finished!"

"Oh, but you are!" someone said, directly behind him.

And then a crushing weight struck him; the light went out of the world and Dal Chantry dropped limply across the body of his enemy.

CHAPTER
TEN

Steve Roman's pale eyes looked coldly down at the man his sixgun barrel had felled. His flat lips quirked into a grimace of amused disgust at the sight of what men could do to one another with their fists — something far removed from Roman's more indirect and devious tactics. The ex-gambler straightened in the saddle then, and let his gunbarrel swing to cover the pair with Chantry.

They sat entirely still, guns in holsters, hands folded on saddle horns. They had put up no argument from the moment Roman and his three Heart Nine riders came onto the scene — apparently they were men who respected odds. Roman said bluntly, "I heard Cross K was hiring crew. I suppose that's who you are . . . What are your names?"

He scarcely listened while they told him. He was looking again, with a crawling distaste, at the figures on the ground. He gestured with the gunbarrel.

"You saw what I had to do to your boss. I think he'd have killed Garrett with his bare hands. When he comes to his senses, I should imagine he'll be glad I stopped him. For now, you'd better put him on his horse and take him away from here."

The two who called themselves Brice and Jennings shared a sullen look and a shrug. Without comment they dismounted and walked over to Dal Chantry, who was already stirring, making some effort to sit up. They each hooked him under an arm and dragged him to his feet, his head hanging. One of Roman's men had caught up the reins of Chantry's black and he rode up leading it. The two Cross K riders half walked, half dragged their boss to his horse and managed — with a little help from Chantry as his head continued to clear — to haul him into the saddle where he sat grasping the horn.

Still without saying a word, they got into their own saddles. Mort Jennings took the reins of the black and they rode away like that, toward the dry wash and the fallen fence line, Jennings leading the black and Ollie Brice riding close to Chantry's stirrup to help hold him from sliding off the back of his horse. The Heart Nine riders watched them go.

Ed Varner, the gunman, had been looking at the place where his sixshooter lay gleaming in the grass. Now, using knee and reins, he sidled his mount over toward it and started to swing out of the saddle. At once the gun in Roman's hand swiveled to a point directly at him, and the gambler said sharply, "Stay where you are!"

Varner flicked him a look, his eyes darkening with surprise and anger — he hadn't expected this. But he shrugged slightly and settled back into the leather, empty-handed, to watch what the gambler would do next.

The latter turned now to Ford Garrett, who had pushed himself to a sit and was crouched with forearms on knees, grizzled head hanging and blood dripping off his battered face onto the grass. Steve Roman eyed him with pure contempt. "I thought you were the man nobody ever beat! That kid sure took you apart."

The foreman's battered head wavered up; he glared at the other.

"Getting a little old for the rough and tumble," Roman suggested, chiding him. "Especially to think you could handle somebody half your age . . ."

"You go to hell!"

But then some of the belligerence faded from Ford Garrett's swollen eyes and was replaced by something else. Roman's face had changed subtly; his voice when he spoke again was softer, colder. "Trouble is," the gambler said, his pale stare drilling into the foreman, "he licked you once, and he can do it again. And he's going to figure he wants to! He'll never be satisfied until he gets to the root of the thing that was done to his partner all those years ago. And where else is the logical place for him to start?"

Garrett scowled, rubbed a palm down over the wreckage of his face and winced at the touch. He said harshly, "He'll get nothing from me. I'll kill him!"

"Maybe," Roman said in the same cool tone. "I'm not sure it's a good risk. He nearly broke you today. I've about decided it isn't worthwhile giving him another chance."

113

The big man went still. Slowly his head lifted; he looked up at the man in the saddle, looming over him. He saw the muzzle of the gun slanted directly down into his face, and his mouth dropped wide and his eyes took on a glint of horror. "No!" he cried hoarsely. "No — no! I never told yet. I never will — !"

"Goodbye, Ford," Steve Roman said, and his wrist jerked to the explosion of the gun.

Garrett was knocked over backward by the slam of the bullet; the horses moved in fright and were pulled down by their riders. With no expression at all in his pale eyes, Steve Roman deliberately swung the gunbarrel back to the gunman, Varner. The latter tore his stare from the murdered foreman to look at the dribble of smoke from the gun that had killed him. His face was sickly gray, but he swallowed and managed to speak.

"You aren't going to shoot me, Roman."

"No? Why not?"

"You need me — to take Ford's body in and tell Luke Blaine and the law how it was the Chantry kid murdered him."

Roman's expression grew thoughtful; the pale eyes narrowed. The gunbarrel wavered and after a moment he lowered it. "Let's hear some more . . ."

Now that he saw the other was interested enough that he didn't intend to shoot him out of hand, the gunman quickly overcame his momentary panic. A breath swelled his chest. He said, promptly, "After the fight, when Chantry rode away promising to finish Garrett, the two of us were heading toward the ranch

114

together when we saw something moving in an alder thicket — looked as if it might be a horse or a steer caught up there. Ford went closer for a look. Just as he got near enough somebody let him have it at point-blank range. By the time I reached him it was too late; but when I went through the brush I saw Chantry running his horse. He'd doubled back and made his threat good."

Steve Roman knuckled his jaw as he narrowly considered the man. "You think you can put that story over and make it stick?" He answered his own question: "Somehow, I think you can. Luke Blaine and that deputy are ready to believe anything against Cross K . . ."

One of his men — a rider named Hilken, the one with the mastiff eyes and the heavy waterfall of moustache — scowled and said darkly, "And after he's hung the frame on Chantry? What does he do then — try to blackmail you from here to doomsday?"

"Do I really look like a fool?" Ed Varner exclaimed quickly.

"There's your answer," Roman told his man. "He knows damned well he'd collect nothing but a bullet." He nodded and, the decision made, shoved his gun into the holster. Lifting the reins, he speared Varner with a cold stare. "All right. You've got your job cut out for you. Do it well and I might have more for you. Come to think of it, it wouldn't hurt at all to have my own man on Luke Blaine's payroll."

"That's what I figured." His confidence restored, Ed Varner lifted his upper lip in something like a smile; it showed all his yellow teeth. "By nightfall," he promised calmly, "Chantry will be in jail for murder — or he'll be a dead man himself. If it's a free hand with Cross K that you're after, you'll have it."

"Never mind what I'm after!" the Heart Nine owner cut him off. "Just prove to me it was worth my while not putting that bullet through your skull!" He turned his horse with a summoning jerk of his head at his three riders. They sent their horses down off the knoll and toward a near line of timber, leaving Varner staring after them with the dead Broken Arrow foreman sprawled in the grass at his feet.

The line storm that had been holding off so long hung like a dense, half-raised curtain now about to descend. It was already storming in the hills, and outriders of the approaching cloud system had moved across the sun, darkening the day and dropping temperatures by degrees. Soon the Oxbow would be engulfed by the smashing, pelting downpour. The wind that ran ahead of it combed the grass and stripped leaves from the cottonwoods, and pushed Dal Chantry around in the saddle as he rode alone toward Cross K.

Except for that pummeling wind he would scarcely have noticed the storm. He had troubles of his own — a dull throbbing of his battered skull, a pain in his lower chest that reminded him, from time to time, of the rib Ford Garrett's heavy boot must have damaged. Brice and Jennings had finally convinced him he should come in and have his hurts tended to.

He was still some distance from ranch headquarters when a rider in a yellow slicker topped out of a tree-choked draw just ahead and held up there as though waiting for him to approach. Caution halted him for an instant, as he tried to make out who it might be. At once that other horseman lifted an arm and signaled with seeming urgency; puzzled, Chantry sent the tired black forward.

To his surprise he saw that the man was Clyde Humbird, mounted on Jess Kingman's sorrel. He appeared upset about something. He swung his arm again in an anxious summons, and afterward turned and dropped the sorrel back into the shelter of the wash. Despite his suspicions of this man, Chantry was curious enough to follow.

As he joined him under the wind-whipped cottonwoods, the Easterner looked into his battered face and exclaimed, "My word! You don't look very good ..." He added quickly, "Where are those two chaps I sent you?"

"They'll be along," Chantry said gruffly. "I left 'em with something to finish up."

"But they've been with you most of the day?" Humbird saw the younger man's puzzled nod, and it seemed to give him some satisfaction. "I thought as much!" he said.

Chantry scowled. "What are you getting at?"

"You have company at the ranch. That deputy fellow, and three others. They're looking for you."

"I got no business with Irv Wallace!"

"He says otherwise." The Easterner's eyes probed Chantry's as he let him have the rest of it: "He wants you, for killing Ford Garrett."

The younger man stared. "I beat the bastard up — but I never hurt him *that* much!"

"It was a bullet killed him. It appears that man Varner claims he saw you do it."

The words burst from Chantry: "He's a liar!"

"Well . . ." The Easterner pursed his lips under the thin moustache. "I admit I'd hesitate to believe much the fellow said. But apparently the deputy does. He's got a warrant with your name on it — and three chaps to help him serve it!"

Dal Chantry could only stare, overwhelmed by this news. Humbird continued. "Millie and I were talking in the kitchen; she answered the door to them. You know," he added with real admiration, "you'd be amazed, the way she handled the situation. I'd somehow thought of her as a timid girl, but she was absolutely cool as ice. Told them to wait a bit and you'd be riding in any time — while I took my cue and went out the back way without letting any of them see me. When I left she was offering them all coffee. Remarkable girl!

"I was hoping to intercept you before you got in. And I saddled a fresh horse, in case you needed one . . ."

The other looked at him sharply. "Are you telling me I got to run for it?"

"I wouldn't presume to advise you. Actually, you don't appear in the best of shape for running. Nevertheless, I felt you should be warned of what's afoot. As it stands, it's your word against Varner's."

"And I know how much of a damn my word is good for!" Dal Chantry took a deep breath. "All right. Let me have the sorrel. I spent too long already looking through steel bars from the wrong side. If they mean to put me there again — for something I didn't do! — they're going to have to catch me."

They made the exchange quickly, Chantry switching his roll to the other saddle. As he swung up wincing against the stab of pain from that damaged rib, Humbird offered him a bundle he'd been carrying across his knees — a black rubber poncho, with some other things wrapped inside. "It looks like a real Montana cloud burst shaping up, and I thought you might not be prepared. There's a little food, too — what I was able to pick up on my way through the kitchen."

Chantry sat a moment staring at this man who stood now, holding the reins of the tired black horse. He blurted finally, "I swear I don't understand you, mister; you and me ain't cut off the same cowhide. I sure never thought you'd go out of your way to do me any favors . . . You sure you ain't making a mistake?"

"You mean, do I think you might have killed Ford Garrett?" Humbird shook his head. "Remember — I was there that day you came storming to Broken Arrow and bearded Luke Blaine on his own veranda. If you were going to kill a man, I think you'd do it in the open and not hiding in the brush."

Dal Chantry grunted, "Thanks." For the first time, he began to think he might be able to like this man.

He lifted the reins. "I better burn some leather."

"Are you certain you're in any condition?" Humbird sounded anxious.

"I'm all right." He squinted thoughtfully in the direction of the hills that were lost in sheets of rain. "Tell Jess and Millie, if they should have to get in touch with me I'll likely be holed up somewhere in the vicinity of Squaw Head. I'll give this thing a chance to shake down a little; by then maybe I'll have some idea of what to do next."

The other nodded. "I'll tell them . . . Good luck, Chantry."

Dal Chantry gave the sorrel the spur and sent it climbing out of the draw, veering north and west away from the ranch and toward the lift of the mountain that enclosed the valley. The buffeting hand of the wind that struck him brought with it the first wet sting of rain. Well, he thought, if he didn't drown or fall from the saddle with exhaustion, at least the storm should help cover his tracks. He pulled up beneath a thick-boled pine long enough to draw the poncho down over his head. He replaced his hat, careful of that aching knot of pain. He had taken up the reins again when he saw something that made him freeze.

Yonder, a quartet of riders had topped a lift in the ground between him and the unseen ranch house. The deputy and his men, he thought — out to look for him! They came on at an easy pace, from which he judged they hadn't seen him yet. As they drew nearer, however, someone was bound to spot him; if he tried to make a break for it, the first move out of the shelter of that pine would give him away. They were on his neck, and escape suddenly looked out of the question.

As he sat debating his hopeless choice, watching those nearing horsemen grow larger against the bunch grass flat, all at once he saw another horse break out of the draw he had left just a moment before. Staring, he lifted in the stirrups; in the same instant he heard a faint yell. The rider in the yellow slicker was spurring at a dead run toward the south, and now those others lifted their mounts to a gallop and peeled away, going after him. Another yell — and the flat crack of hand guns began.

"Why, the damned fool!" Chantry exclaimed.

The black had already put in a solid day's work — it couldn't hope to outrace the deputy's men; before they could learn that the rider wasn't the man they wanted, there was every chance that one of those hasty bullets would find a target. Chantry held his breath as he watched the chase move away from him, wincing at each crack of a gunshot that rode back upon the wind. After that, pursuers and pursued had swept from sight in a belt of timber and he lowered himself into the saddle leather again, finding his limbs shaky with fatigue and tension.

Well, there was not a damn thing he could do to help Clyde Humbird. Meanwhile the Easterner had deliberately taken a big risk, simply to give him a chance to escape; it would be poor payment to waste the effort. Reluctantly, and with all his thoughts still pinned on that frantic chase that had moved now

121

beyond his sight and hearing, he turned the sorrel and started again toward the rain-shrouded hills.

CHAPTER
ELEVEN

It was with a curse and an involuntary jerk of the leathers that Dal Chantry brought the sorrel to a stand. Morning sun, in a sky hung with tatters of the night's storm, spilled its heat into this blind canyon where barren rock walls collected it as in a cup. A buzz of flies was in the stillness, and the smell of the place turned the horse restless and collected in Chantry's throat so that he had to fight to keep from gagging.

He counted again . . . seventeen. Predators had been at them, and what was left of the carcasses was bloated and rotting almost beyond recognition, but there was no question — he'd found, at last, the jag of missing Broken Arrow cattle that had been the cause of the argument with Ford Garrett, the one in which Jess Kingman had been shot.

Someone had taken the trouble to drive the beef up here and slaughter them in pure and senseless malice. So far as Chantry could see, it couldn't have been for any other purpose than simply to make trouble. No use looking for clues, not after time and weather had washed away all sign as effectively as — he hoped — his own tracks would have been lost in last night's storm. He reined away, as pleased as the sorrel to get out of this cul-de-sac of death that he had stumbled upon quite by accident.

All around him, rocks and tree trunks steamed as sunlight drank up the moisture; he, too, was drying out after a miserable night when he had been unable to find real shelter, and even the poncho had been unable to keep him dry. He had never had much chance to get familiar with these hills and he was riding blind now. However, with the passing of the cloud wrack that had held the peaks in hiding he was able to see the granite dome of Squaw Head. This was a dominating landmark and he worked his way steadily toward it, following game trails and always keeping a watch for any sign of a manhunt.

Once, from a vantage point, he was certain he caught a glimpse of a line of horsemen threading a way through the timber not far below; it gave him a bad five minutes until he got another look and saw it was merely a buck deer and a pair of does. He could not have believed it possible a posse would be this close behind him . . .

Not far below the bare rock shoulder of the Head, he found a natural overhang with a growth of scrub pine for a screen and even, not too far away, a spring bubbling up ice-cold into a stony basin. Here, he thought, his camp would be safe enough and he could afford the luxury of a fire. He stored his belongings beneath the overhang and put the sorrel, still saddled, out on a patch of grass. With luck, he located some dry wood and toted a supply into his shelter.

All that accomplished, he sat down to wait — and futility and rank impatience took hold of him.

What earthly good was he doing himself here, he wondered. Like a caged panther, he prowled hopelessly back and forth behind the imprisoning bars of his futile thoughts. He should be accomplishing something — seeking a way to clear himself of the murder charge in Ford Garrett's death. Instead of that, all he could say was that he was sitting up here in the clean open and not in that smelly jail in Oxbow. If worse came to worst and the hunters got too near, he supposed he could follow this spine of the Rockies the few miles north to the Canada line. Rather than face capture, he would do just that. But he knew perfectly well that would turn him into a fugitive and leave the Kingmans to face their enemies alone. And everything in Dal Chantry's nature rebelled at the thought.

It was a little past noon and inactivity had brought him to this point in his bitter and useless brooding, when the distant trumpeting of a horse came to him, faintly but unmistakably. It was a startling sound and it brought him rolling to his feet, so hastily that a stab of pain from that injured rib left him gasping, with a hand clasped to his side.

He had decided the rib was not too seriously damaged, and the hurt in his skull where Steve Roman's gunbarrel had struck him down was now little more than an occasional throbbing ache. He ignored both now as he came ducking out from under the overhang and stood listening for a repetition of the horse sound. It didn't come, but he knew he hadn't imagined it; it couldn't be ignored for it meant at least one other rider in the hills. Naturally his first thought was of Deputy Wallace and a posse.

His sixgun, he found, was in his hand without his being aware of pulling it. Still carrying the weapon, he started to work his way to a point where he would have a better view over the fall of timber and running ridges that stepped away from his front door.

The last of the cloud wrack had long since burned away and the air was crystal clear. From here he could see other hills, like blue curtains, that marked the eastern edge of Oxbow Valley, and even some glimpse of the rangeland in between. Nearer, the forest was like a deep-napped carpet, broken by upthrust spines of bare granite and the occasional open of mountain meadow. A hawk rode motionless with spread wings on some column of heated air; otherwise Chantry saw nothing move and heard nothing except the murmur of wind in the pines in back of him.

Then his eye was caught by a tiny clearing to the south which held the deep blue stain of a small mountain lake. A trail, marked out by game and livestock, touched the lake and then moved from sight again into the nearer trees. Simply because it was a trail — something made by living beings — Chantry's eye held on it for a moment; and now, without warning, a pair of riders broke out of the timber and came down to the edge of the water, where they paused to let their horses drink.

He could wish then that he had a pair of field glasses. Without them, and for all the clarity of the summer day, it was just too far down there to identify a rider without them. Still, the horses — a brown and a buckskin — looked familiar, and so did the red-and-black checkered shirt on one of the men. Suddenly Chantry decided he knew who they were.

They were pulling away from the lake now, following that trail along its bank. Chantry didn't wait to see the nearer trees swallow them; he was already turning, hurrying back to the place where he had staked out his horse. He rose to the saddle and put the sorrel down a dim track and into a draw choked with twinkling aspens. Minutes later he dropped out of the lower mouth of the draw, turned south to climb a spur ridge and then quartered down the far side, through the pines. Here caution warned him to hold up where the trees gave him some cover. He waited.

Sounds came to him — a drift of voices, the ring of an iron shoe striking rock. Then, where the faint stock trail broke around the shoulder of a ridge some hundred yards above and to the right of him, Ollie Brice and Mort Jennings rode into view at an easy walk, one behind the other.

They were talking as they rode; Brice, forking the buckskin in the lead, had just said something that amused him and he was turned in the saddle to look at his companion, thick shoulders shaking with laughter. Neither seemed to notice Chantry until they were almost upon him, and he edged the sorrel out of the tree shadows and said, "Were you fellows looking for me?"

The blond man whipped about, his mouth sagging, face ludicrous with surprise. "Hey!" he exclaimed. "Hey, Mort! Here's the kid!"

Jennings pulled up even with him as he dragged on the reins. Red-lashed eyes in the narrow, fox-like face studied Chantry. "Looks like you're really on the watch," he told Chantry. "We been riding blind. All Humbird could tell us was to make toward that Squaw Head peak."

"Then Humbird's all right, I guess?" Chantry was surprised at the intense feeling of relief it gave him. "Last I saw of him, he was riding the other way to pull Irv Wallace and a posse off me — and getting shot at!"

"Is that a fact?" The two exchanged a look. "He never told us *that* part," Ollie Brice said. "But I never seen no mark on him, so I guess they must not have tagged him." His lips spread in a grin under the pale moustache. "Hey! I bet that squint-eyed deputy must of been fit to be tied, when he seen how he got tricked — and by a dude!"

Relieved though he might be, Chantry was in no mood to make a joke of it. He broke in crisply, "I hope you haven't gone and let a posse trail you up here."

"You think we ain't got any sense?" The grin turned to a scowl. "We had our eyes open, kid. And we never seen nobody."

"You never saw *me*, either — till you were right on top of me! I'd say that was pretty damned careless. What did you come for, anyway?"

Under his probing stare, the two of them seemed taken aback. "If you want to know," Mort Jennings retorted, "we were trying to be helpful." The redhead indicated a canvas sack lashed behind his saddle. "Humbird said you didn't have much in the way of supplies. We volunteered to bring you up some more."

"Oh . . ." Chantry felt a twinge of guilt, a sense that he owed some gratitude toward this pair who, after all, were doing what they could to make up for the blunder four years ago at Miles. He scowled and nodded as he said gruffly, "All right, I'm sorry. Guess I'm just too damned anxious about saving my neck."

"Sure." The affable grin was back on Ollie Brice's dark features. He looked around. "Where you camped, kid?"

The fugitive shook his head. "What you don't know, you can't be made to tell. And I don't want you coming up here again unless it's absolutely necessary. There's too much risk."

The two riders shared a look. Then Mort Jennings shrugged inside the red-and-black checked shirt. "If that's how you want it," he said, and turned to unfasten the lashings of the canvas sack.

Chantry accepted it and laid it across his knees. Afterward the three of them sat looking at one another in a strange, expectant silence in which a hum of insects and the squawking of a jay somewhere in the near timber were oddly magnified. Chantry had a sudden feeling that these other two were waiting for him to turn and ride away, and for some reason he was just as determined to let them make the first move. They did, finally — Mort Jennings picking up the reins and saying roughly, with a jerk of the head to his towheaded companion, "Well — let's go, then. It's a far piece down from here."

Ollie Brice opened his mouth, closed it again. The redhead was already turning his horse and starting up that draw toward the ridge shoulder; scowling, Brice fell in behind him. And now Dal Chantry, seeing them on their way, spoke to the sorrel and started his turn to reenter the timber.

Some sound gave him warning. He kicked the sorrel hard, still holding him on short rein; and so came on around in a complete, tight circle. As he did he heard Ollie Brice's shout: "Damn it — *get him!*"

A gunshot exploded in the stillness; the bullet struck a pine branch overhead and splattered him with bark and needles. Chantry's own gun was already sliding into his hand; yonder, he saw Ollie Brice lowering his smoking sixgun for another try. Mort Jennings was hunched over a saddlegun, working the lever to bring a shell under the firing pin.

There was no time to think. Chantry thumbed off a shot and missed, the sound of the guns running together. The sorrel was having trouble with the slick forest litter underfoot; now a bullet from the rifle thudded into it and knocked the animal to its knees. Chantry felt it going and kicked out of the stirrups. He landed free, but he hit hard and the pain of that damaged rib stunned him. Still, he managed to lift his gun from the ground and in prone position flung a bullet at Jennings as the latter cranked the lever of the carbine.

The redhead seemed to throw the rifle away and went over the tail of his horse in a sprawling tumble. Ollie Brice, his face a mask of fury, was standing in the stirrups and holding his bronc under control with one hand while he worked the sixshooter with the other. The horse's wild maneuverings under him hampered his aim but also interfered with Chantry's attempt to find a target. Now, trying to rise, he found his legs entangled with the limp, half-filled supply sack. Desperately he kicked free of it and then simply rolled, bringing up against a rotted log. Half propped there, he lifted his gun. He found the face with the straggling yellow moustache above his sights, and he worked the trigger just as Ollie fired again.

Powdersmoke whipped across his face in a stinking fog; as it cleared and the last echoes of gunfire went rocketing off through the hills, he saw the brown horse on the slope had an empty saddle.

The stillness returned — more complete now, because the jay had taken off at the outbreak of shooting. Slowly Chantry climbed to his feet. The sorrel lay dead where it had gone down; the other pair of horses had wandered off a little before they fell to cropping the thin wire grass. Marveling a little that no bullet had touched him in all that frantic, wild exchange, Chantry walked across to where the men he had shot lay crumpled.

Jennings was dead and Chantry went on to Ollie Brice. The man lay on his back, fighting for breath. Chantry's bullet had taken him in the chest; his face was a sick gray color. As Chantry dropped to one knee the blond rider twisted his head around for a look at him. His voice came as a painful whisper.

"By God! I told Mort — it would take both of us. And then we still couldn't make it . . ."

"Even though you waited till my back was turned." But you couldn't berate a dying man, and Dal Chantry shook his head in complete bewilderment. "I just don't understand! *Why?* Why did you do it? For what possible reason?"

"Reason?" The lips twisted in a grotesque parody of the man's familiar, mocking grin. "I guess we forgot to tell you: Luke Blaine's offering five hundred dollars — for the man who killed his foreman. We figured, if we didn't collect it, somebody would . . ."

The words broke off. The dying man's chest swelled, he coughed hideously and a flow of blood dribbled from his mouth. When he went limp he seemed to collapse upon himself, and the eyes rolled sightlessly beneath the upper lids.

Ollie Brice was as dead as he would ever be.

CHAPTER
TWELVE

Considerably shaken, Chantry climbed to his feet and stood looking at the crumpled bodies. There was bitter irony in the thought that these two men, who would have betrayed and killed him for the sake of a five hundred dollar reward, were the nearest to friends he had ever had, in a short and chaotic lifetime.

But then he thought, *No — not these!* Brice and Jennings were a part of the past — of the random, wasted years that were best forgotten. He had some real friends now: Jess and Millie Kingman, Ada Starbuck. Yes, and he even had to count Clyde Humbird, who'd deliberately risked his life yesterday helping him escape . . .

Meanwhile he had problems. The dead men were easily disposed of — there was a brush-choked draw handy and he gingerly set about hauling them into it, one after the other, and stowing them out of sight under dead brush and branches. This was a distasteful job and he was glad when it was finished; he supposed that predators would be after the bodies, but he could do nothing about that. What was more important, he had no way at all of hiding the carcass of the sorrel. It would lie there, a sure guidepost to the posse when they

133

stumbled across it, as they were bound to eventually. It would tell them he had been in this vicinity, and so his hideout under the ledge was no further use to him.

He would have to catch up one of the extra horses and move on. Actually it didn't make much difference. His patience was shot with the amount of futile sitting still he'd already done.

Leaning for the carbine Mort Jennings had dropped as he died, he caught a movement down on the open flat to his left. Almost without thinking, he spun and sank to one knee as he flipped the lever. His sights quickly found and settled upon the figure of a single rider; then with a sudden exclamation he snatched the carbine down from his shoulder, nearly dropping it. He stayed where he was a moment, making sure there were no other horsemen in the flickering aspens. Slowly he rose to his feet and started down the slope, swinging the carbine above his head in greeting. A raised hand answered his signal, and Gwen Macaulay lifted her pony in a lope and came to meet him.

She was dressed as he had first seen her that night he arrived on the Oxbow — in a blouse and riding habit, her fair hair caught up beneath the brim of a flat-topped riding hat. She dropped from the saddle and caught at his hand, and her touch felt cold. She exclaimed, "Are you all right? I heard gunfire . . ."

Briefly he told her what had happened, and was astonished at the way her cheeks paled with alarm. "Your own riders!" she said. "Oh, how terrible!"

"They weren't much," he said, bitterly. "Your uncle's reward looked pretty big to them, I guess."

134

Her face fell; her hand dropped away from his. "You don't know how awful I feel! I mean, about the reward." She shook her head. "I've tried, but there's no reasoning with Uncle Luke since Mr. Garrett was killed."

"No reason for you to apologize. What makes you so sure I didn't kill him?"

She dismissed that. "What makes a person sure of a lot of things? I just am!" She looked into his face. "And I want to help. There's a posse in here looking for you — but I think I must know these hills better than almost anyone. I've spent a lot of time riding them, during this past year."

Chantry asked bluntly, "Does Clyde Humbird know what you're up to?"

"I didn't tell him. He'd have tried to talk me out of it. He'd say it was dangerous."

"And he'd be right! Did you know he came near getting killed yesterday, helping me to get away?"

She stared. "No! He didn't tell me . . ." As she thought about it she put up a hand, in an unconsciously graceful movement, to push a tendril of hair back beneath her hatbrim. "But I can believe it," she said, nodding. "It's so like him."

"Yeah." Gruffly. "I almost wish he hadn't. It's no fun having to like somebody you're jealous of."

The girl frowned. "You're jealous of him? I hope it's not because he has money."

"No. It's because he has you!"

"*Me?*"

He looked away from her wide-eyed gaze, ashamed at having blurted it out. His fingers were clamped hard on the balance of the rifle he still carried. "Forget it! Makes no sense, anyway — jailbait scum even letting himself think about something as far above him and so far out of his reach! Besides, I ain't forgetting what I stumbled onto out on the porch, that night Humbird come to make Jess and me his offer."

"I kissed him!" she breathed. "You saw that — but you didn't know why it happened. I had just told him what he suspected all along — that I liked and admired him, but it could never be anything more than that . . ."

Dal Chantry blinked. "Do you only kiss men when you're feeling sorry for them?"

She smiled at that. "There's no need to feel sorry for Clyde Humbird. The last few days he's had eyes for only one person — your friend Millie Kingman. And I don't think he's mistaken: she's very sweet and she has a real inner strength. In a way they're very much alike. And I'm happy for both of them."

But Chantry scarcely heard. "But even if it isn't Humbird, with you," he blurted, "that surely don't mean there'd ever be a chance for — ?"

"I like a man who makes his own chances," Gwen told him. "A man who asks no advantages from life, but simply stands up and fights for his place and his rights. There weren't too many such men in that world I left a year ago. Yet I've always known if he came my way — I could love someone like that . . ."

Her words ended, but the promise and meaning of them thundered in his ears. Unheeded, the rifle slid from his hand with a clatter. His hands fumbled, reaching for her; then, incredibly, she was in his arms and his mouth found hers.

Abruptly he released her, stepping back. "This is crazy!" he cried hoarsely. "Damn it, I'm on the run — with a murder charge hanging over my head!"

"But you're innocent!" She came close again and seized his arm. "Don't you see, that makes all the difference — because there must surely be a way to prove it!"

He started to shake his head, then didn't; slowly he lifted a hand, ran it across his face that held the marks of fatigue and of his brutal fight with Luke Blaine's foreman. There was a sudden subtle change in his manner.

"You know," he said slowly, "there just might be a way! One man is the key to this situation — God knows, I've had plenty of time to figure that out since yesterday; I've thought of hardly anything else! But with my own neck in a sling I couldn't see much chance of doing anything about it.

"Still, if that man's not running with the posse — and somehow I doubt it — then I know where he will be: at Broken Arrow." He nodded, seeing the girl's look. "That's right. At your uncle's spread — where, until this minute, I couldn't see I had a prayer of getting at him. But if you're willing to help me —"

She nodded quickly. Chantry leaned and picked up the rifle he'd dropped. "I'll grab me a horse and we'll head for low country. And just hope that posse doesn't see us before we see them!"

In moments of idleness, Ed Varner's hands went instinctively to his sixshooter. It was the essential tool of his trade and he never felt satisfied that it was in proper condition. Now as he sat on a bench in the shadow of the bunkhouse wall, the ranch yard beyond swimming in afternoon heat, he plucked the weapon from its well-oiled holster and put it through a routine inspection: searching for nonexistent particles of dust, trying the pull of the hammer spring, and finally — one by one — pulling the loads and examining each bullet as he turned it in his dry, lean fingers. One failed to satisfy him for some reason; he tossed it aside and replaced it from a loop of his cartridge belt. He spun the cylinder, settling the empty chamber beneath the firing pin. And then he looked up as hoofbeats struck the hardpan of the Broken Arrow yard.

It was the Macaulay girl. She came down out of the aspens on the slope behind the ranch, moving in past the breaking corral and the blacksmith shop, where a couple of Blaine's punchers were shoeing horses, and quartered across the yard to a halt directly in front of Varner. She swung lightly down and dropped the reins. She said, "Will you take care of him, please? You'd better rub him down and give him some grain."

Varner looked at her and at the horse. The bay needed attention; it shone with sweat and looked to have had a good workout. But why put the job on him? He couldn't remember her wasting so much as half a dozen words on him all the months he'd been here, and there were other riders handy, even if a lot of the crew

138

were out hunting that Chantry bastard. Either of that pair at the smithy would like as not been only too glad to drop their work and jump to her bidding.

He put all his dislike into the coldly insolent stare he gave her, but then he got to his feet, dropping the gun back into its holster. "All right," he said shortly, and reached for the reins.

After all, he had to be cautious. With Ford Garrett dead, his own position at Broken Arrow was not yet clear. He had been Garrett's man, not Blaine's. If Blaine's niece should accuse him to her uncle of acting with disrespect, it wasn't out of the question that the arrogant sonofabitch would get sore and boot him off the spread and thus ruin his deal to act as spy for Steve Roman. And so, swallowing his resentments, he went off toward the barn, leading the bay. Once he glanced back and saw the girl staring after him and it seemed to him she looked oddly white and tense. He briefly wondered about that, then dismissed her with a shrug of his narrow, sloping shoulders.

He walked into the musty coolness of the barn.

In this booming quiet, his own footsteps and the clomp of the bay's shod hooves covered all smaller sounds; he suspected nothing until a shadow moved suddenly in a stall as he passed it, and he felt a slight tug at his holster. Ed Varner spun, dropping the reins and slashing a hand toward his gun — just in time to feel it slide away from under his fingers. He stood staring, helpless and disarmed, into the muzzle of his own revolver, and then into the shadowed face of the man who held it.

He suddenly felt all the juices dry out of his throat and the hard bands of fear squeezed with an iron tightness about his chest. Dal Chantry said, "Hello, Varner."

The gunman found his voice. "How the hell did you get in here?" And then it came to him: "*She* put you here — and then sent me in to you! I should have known the bitch was up to something!" He broke off as he saw the quick flare of anger in those other eyes, the way the gunbarrel lifted as though Chantry meant to strike him with it. He swallowed his words as a cold bath of sweat broke out on him.

"Watch your tongue!" the man with the gun snapped coldly. "I won't take much off of you!"

Varner said hoarsely, "I dunno what you think you're trying to get away with! There's men all around this yard. Not a one of 'em but will shoot to kill, if they lay eyes on you."

"I'll worry about that. Right now it's you I'm talking to."

Defiantly: "I've done all my talking — to the sheriff's office!"

"I reckon we'll see about that!" Chantry's eyes narrowed thoughtfully. "You know, I got a theory about men like you — men that depend on their guns. I always figured, take their guns away and they'd cave pretty quick. I think I'll find out!" Deliberately he tossed the captured weapon across the wooden partition into a stall and, curling his big hands into fists, he moved in on the gunman.

Ed Varner opened his mouth to yell for help and took a blow that mashed his lips and drove him stumbling back against a roof prop. The bay horse snorted uneasily and backed away a step. Half blinded, Varner struck out and caught his tormentor low in the rib cage and thought he saw a flicker of agony cross the other man's face. But he had no chance to work on that, for Chantry was crowding him unmercifully. Pinned against the timber, he took a numbing drive in the chest and then a hard fist opened his cheek. Agony lit a fire all through him. He heard a voice, suddenly pleading; it was his own.

Dal Chantry found that the blooming pain in his own middle was no more than he could handle without interfering with what he had to do. Fists clenched and ready, he said in a voice without warmth, "Do you still say I killed Garrett?"

The man stood against the roof prop, doubled forward slightly. Incredibly, pain and the fear of pain seemed already to have broken him; when he spoke it was with an effort, as though he fought to keep from retching: "Maybe — maybe I was wrong about who I saw ride out of that thicket . . ."

"I don't think there was any thicket," Chantry said inexorably. "I think you made it all up. Maybe you killed him yourself!"

"No — no!" The frightened man recoiled in panic. "Not me! It was Steve Roman!"

"Roman?" Chantry snapped. "You expect me to believe that? It was Roman nearly busted my skull, hauling me off him!"

"It's still the truth, whether you believe me or not!" Varner's voice was mounting in volume, taking on an edge of hysteria. "I was there, I tell you. I seen it! Then he made me agree to tell a yarn to the deputy . . ."

"Why? Where do you come into this?"

"I don't come into it at all — except I was on Broken Arrow's payroll, and now I'm on Heart Nine's. All I know besides that is what I heard Garrett spill one night when he'd had too much likker."

Chantry said, "Keep talking. What did you hear?"

Now that he had started, he seemed only too glad to talk rather than face more punishment from those hard fists. "It goes back twelve years, to the time Garrett ran across Roman and some of his friends running off a jag of Broken Arrow beef to sell in Canada. Garrett owed Steve a bundle on gambling losses; Steve said if he'd forget what he'd seen and put the blame on Jess Kingman — then he'd tear up the notes and call it square. Otherwise, Garrett was as good as a dead man!"

Chantry felt the ache of clenched muscles in his jaw. "But why lay it to Kingman? What could a tinhorn like Steve Roman have against a man who'd never done him any hurt?"

"That I don't know!" The gunman shook his head emphatically, almost babbling. "Chantry, I swear I don't! Neither did Garrett — but he figured he had no choice but go along. You don't cross Steve Roman, I don't care who you are! You do just what he —"

The hurried voice broke off. The man was staring past Chantry toward the door of the barn, and the latter quickly wheeled.

142

Luke Blaine's blocky shape stood silhouetted against the fading sunset glow of the yard outside. In his fist a hogleg revolver gleamed faintly, leveled at them both. "So!" the Broken Arrow boss said. And deliberately he walked forward.

There was a sudden cry, and Gwen came hurrying into the barn to clutch at her uncle's arm — pleading with him, trying to halt his inexorable stride. She was half sobbing. "No! Please! You mustn't do it! Didn't you hear *any* of what they've been saying? Didn't you *hear?*" Never taking his eyes or his gun from the pair in front of him, the big man merely shook free; Gwen sagged against the rough wall, shoulders drooping, and dropped her face into her hands. Luke Blaine kept coming.

Even if he had wanted to try for the gun in his holster, Dal Chantry knew it would have been futile against that leveled revolver. He could merely wait with fists clenched as the Broken Arrow owner came to a solid stand. The rancher's face was terrible with anger as he looked from one to the other, and Dal Chantry braced himself for whatever was to come.

Then, without a word, Blaine raised his arm and swept a backhand blow across Ed Varner's face and knocked him sprawling in the straw and filth of the barn floor. "You scum!" he gritted. Turning to Chantry, swinging his heavy shoulders, he added in a rough voice: "Yeah, I heard. I heard plenty! Enough to make a man's hide fairly crawl with shame!"

Knees suddenly gone weak, Chantry could only stare back at him while, yonder, Gwen watched them both in astonished silence. At their feet Ed Varner — the inscrutable, the dangerous, the cold-eyed Ed Varner — lay whimpering like a kicked pup . . .

CHAPTER
THIRTEEN

Millie Kingman was frying up a steak for her father's supper, and the sizzling and pop of grease in the pan was the only sound she was aware of. It must have been some instinctive warning of other eyes watching her that made her turn suddenly toward the door separating kitchen and living room. When she saw the man standing silently there, she couldn't repress a start and a gasp.

Apparently her reaction amused him. The smoothshaven cheeks with their patterns of tiny blood vessels broke in a smile. In his passage through the living room, Steve Roman had dropped his hat upon' the center table; now he ran a palm across his receding hairline, smoothing it, and said, "I didn't mean to startle you, my dear. The door was open and I could see you didn't hear my knock."

"No. I didn't." She managed that much, and then the words seemed to get jammed against the fear that clogged her throat. She stood by the stove and stared at him. When the grease in the frying pan began to smoke she reached, almost automatically, and pushed it away from the fire.

Roman came a step further into the room. "Your father's asleep?"

"He'll be waking any minute," she said quickly, "and wanting his supper. I'll be glad to call him —"

She had begun edging toward the door but he stopped her with a raised hand. "I wouldn't think of it." He looked around the quiet kitchen. Outside the window, the last light of a summer evening was quickly fading. Roman said, "I see that dude, Humbird, isn't around, either — though I've noticed he seems to be spending more and more of his time here, and I've wondered why. And of course young Chantry definitely won't be showing up." His smile broadened. "So nobody's going to care if you and I were to have a little talk . . ."

Staring at him, she could only ask herself again what it was about this man that so repelled and terrified her. It wasn't alone the piercing paleness of his eyes, the odd sense he somehow gave of being physically dirty. There was something else — something she couldn't analyze — that set her to stammering wordlessly and circling to put the table between them. At that the pale eyes narrowed, the smile took on an edge.

"Now, now!" he chided. "You're not letting on that there's some reason you'd rather not be alone with me?" Without any warning, he reached across the table and seized her by one bare arm. "Why, do you know, your flesh is like ice."

Suddenly, with a fear that was purely nauseous, she was fighting to break loose. When he finally had to let her go, she backed away with her blue eyes pinned to his face — and containing a blinding, complete understanding. "I know you!" she cried. "It was *you!* You're the man!"

"I am?" His eyes watched her carefully. "I wonder if you think you know what you're talking about!"

"I couldn't be mistaken!" she cried. "Even if I *was* only a little girl! I was sitting right there on the floor, playing with my dolls." She flung a pointing hand. "Mother and I were alone. And someone came to the door . . ."

The words seemed to pour from her now, as Steve Roman stood watching her white face. "They talked for a while. Being a child, I really didn't pay much attention — until suddenly I heard my mother scream. She and this man were struggling. She must have raked his cheek with her nails because he suddenly let her go and stumbled back, and my mother whirled and got the loaded rifle off its pegs on the wall.

"I stood petrified with fright. I've never seen anything so terrible as the man's face as he looked at the rifle; and I'll never forget what he said, then: 'You'll be sorry for this, every day of your life!'" A shudder went through her and she closed her eyes a moment — and opened them again to see, still before her, those pale eyes that had laid buried in her nightmares. "Oh, I *should* have known you the moment I saw you again. Except you've changed. You're so much older . . ."

The eyes hardened. "Not that much older!" he snapped. "But *you!*" he added, drawing a step closer. "Do you realize, you've grown to be the perfect image of that black-haired bitch who dared to turn up her nose and use her claws and a rifle on me? I promised her she'd regret it, and she did! I sent her husband to prison and when she still refused me, I drove her away from the Oxbow — away from my sight, where she could never torment me again. But — here *you* are: that woman, to the life! The same face, the same —"

The glitter of his eyes failed to warn her in time. Suddenly he was upon her. One hand trapped her wrists and hauled her, screaming and struggling, against him. The other sank its lean, gambler's fingers into the black mass of her hair, bent her head back until her frantic look met the eyes bent close above her. "By God!" Steve Roman panted. "*This* time —"

A hand fell upon his shoulder, tried to pull him about. An angry voice shouted. Steve Roman was startled into a quick turn, and the girl broke free and stumbled against a chair, overturning it. In the doorway behind Roman, Jess Kingman stood braced on bare feet, a flannel nightshirt dangling at his bare shanks, his whole body trembling with the exertion that turned his face ashen. Pain and fury twisted his face and shook his voice. "*This* time," he cried, "you're going to pay — for what you've done to me and mine!"

"You think so?" The gambler sneered. "You're twelve years too late to do the job. You're nothing but the wreck of a man!"

Despite a half-healed bullet wound, Jess Kingman hurled himself upon his enemy.

With contemptuous ease Roman flung him aside, and then a clubbing blow of one fist struck the older man and spun him, driving him against the doorway

148

casing. Kingman slammed into it hard, spilled through and down to a limp sprawl on the floor of the living room beyond. And Millie, choking out a scream as the blow was struck, slipped past Kingman's assailant and flung herself on her knees beside her father.

He lay like one dead, the whites of his eyes showing beneath the lids. "Pa! Oh, Pa!" Sobbing, Millie clutched at him but could get no response. She lifted blazing eyes. "You've killed him!"

"I doubt it." Roughly the gambler caught her by an arm and hauled her up. "Now quiet down or I'll give you something to really make you yell!"

She struck at him; her fist barely glanced off his cheekbone but it stung a curse from the man and she was able to tear free of his fingers. She retreated before him, then turned and bolted in blind flight toward the open door and the refuge of gathering dusk.

Outside she almost ran headlong into a bronc that was just being pulled to a stop before the porch. She saw the loom of the muscled shoulder, caught the gleam of an eyeball as the animal tossed its head. Her quick recoil nearly threw her into the path of a second mount and it whinnied shrilly; its rider gave a startled yell. Terrified and confused then, Millie Kingman stood helpless with palms pressed to cheeks as, for a frightening moment, the world seemed to her filled with the lunge and trample of horses trying to run her down.

Then they settled and a familiar and welcome voice spoke her name. A hand touched her shoulder. "Millie! What's going on?"

"Dal!" she cried. "Dal, it's that Steve Roman. He —"

Chantry swore and then he was spurring straight toward the house just as the figure of the gambler showed, silhouetted against the dim light of the doorway. Chantry shouted at him: "Roman, we're taking you! Ed Varner talked. We know you murdered Garrett . . ."

The Heart Nine owner dived quickly sideward, out of the doorway and into the piled shadows of the porch. At the same moment a gun was in his hand; he fired, shooting upward at the man in the saddle.

Chantry's shot answered him, the reports mingling, the fingers of muzzle-flame crossing each other in the gloom. Chantry was pulling hard on the reins then, holding back his mount before it could try to climb the porch; one shod hoof actually struck the wood and it snorted and backed off a nervous step.

Steve Roman's gun roared a second time, but that must have been a final crimping spasm of his finger on the trigger. His bullet thudded into the boards at his feet, and after that there was the loose, thudding collapse of his body hitting the floorboards.

A moment of stillness then was broken by the uneasy stirring of the restless horses. Luke Blaine's question cut through the quiet. "Is he dead, Chantry?"

"I reckon." A step up onto the porch, a brief examination, confirmed it. "He's dead, all right."

Saddle leather creaked as Blaine and the two punchers he had brought with him came down from their horses. Gwen Macaulay had already dismounted to throw a comforting arm about Millie Kingman, who was quietly weeping. Millie said in a muffled voice, "I'm all right. But I don't know about Pa —"

At once Dal Chantry was hurrying into the house, Blaine at his heels. Jess Kingman lay motionless before the kitchen doorway; with an oath Chantry bent to look at him, then gathered him up and carried him in and laid him on his bunk, while Luke Blaine got the lamp on the bedside table to burning.

Kingman was rallying, with an almost frantic note in his voice as he tried to struggle up, crying his daughter's name. Chantry restrained him. "She's fine, Jess. And Roman's took care of, if that's what bothers you."

Kingman sank back, eased by this assurance. Big Luke Blaine, scowling uncomfortably, moved his weight from one foot to the other as he growled, "A damn good thing we stopped by! We were on our way to Heart Nine — but I wanted a word with you, Kingman. Wanted to tell you I know, now, what a damn fool I let that bastard make out of me in his scheming against you. Even after you went to prison, I can remember now that it must have been him started the talk about your wife, that ended with her being driven away from the Oxbow. I only wish to God —"

Dal Chantry interrupted roughly. "That can wait. Maybe it eases your conscience to apologize, Blaine, but I don't think he wants to listen to you right now. He'd rather Ada Starbuck was here. I think that bullet wound may have been reopened . . ."

At once Blaine started from the room, pausing at the door long enough to add, "You'll be seeing me again,

151

Kingman. We'll straighten things out." Then he was tramping through the house and they could hear him yelling at his punchers: "Throw that carcass across his saddle, take him in to town and tell Irv Wallace the manhunt for Chantry is off. And one of you bring Ada Starbuck out here . . ."

Alone, Chantry looked down at his partner. "You just take it easy now. You'll see — the old Oxbow don't have to be the bitter kind of valley it's been for you. Everything's finally going to be all right."

Jess Kingman's head moved on the pillow; a smile softened the pain-tight furrows of his cheeks. "Why, sure, boy," he murmured. "Didn't I always tell you that?"

He closed his eyes, still smiling. Chantry left him there and stepped into the other room to find both girls anxiously waiting for a sign. He nodded gravely — and in Gwen's eyes read her answering look of warmth and promise.